Praise for Michelle M. Pillow's
Realm Immortal: Stone Queen

5 Klovers! "When many authors would have been satisfied with a pat little happy ending for a couple, Pillow revisits them with a realistic approach to love and relationships, proving by example to her readers that 'Happy Ever Afters' do not just happen, they must be worked for and maintained."

~ *Jennifer, Kwips and Kritiques*

4 1/2 Kisses! "Realm Immortal: Stone Queen is a detailed fantasy romance... Rich in detail and genealogy, many characters are included and all are well-delineated. The plot is rapid and keeps the reader's attention right through the story."

~ *Two Lips Reviews*

4 Angels! "Michelle M. Pillow has created a fantastic series overflowing with magic and a plot so thick I found myself rereading different chapters to make sure I hadn't missed a thing. Lovers of Ms. Pillow's work will enjoy her latest book as it is enchanting and full of everything needed to keep you coming back for more."

~ *Rachelle, Fallen Angel Reviews*

Realm Immortal: Stone Queen

Michelle M. Pillow

A Samhain Publishing, Ltd. publication.

Samhain Publishing, Ltd.
512 Forest Lake Drive
Warner Robins, GA 31093
www.samhainpublishing.com

Realm Immortal: Stone Queen
Copyright © 2007 by Michelle M. Pillow
Print ISBN: 1-59998-640-X
Digital ISBN: 1-59998-433-4

Editing by Angie James
Cover by Scott Carpenter

First Samhain Publishing, Ltd. electronic publication: March 2007
First Samhain Publishing, Ltd. print publication: October 2007

Dedication

To 'B', for more reasons than could ever be written in words. You are destined for great things. I love you infinity plus one.

Note from Author:

Though they can be read separately, there are underlying, continual themes within the Realm Immortal stories. The author recommends reading the books in order of release for full entertainment value. For details or reading order please visit her website (www.michellepillow.com).

Main Cast of Characters

King Merrick of the Unblessed

High King of the Kingdom of Valdis, Ruler of the Necessary Evil. He lives in the Black Palace. Having kidnapped the mortal ward of his estranged brother, King Ean of the Blessed, Merrick later made Lady Juliana of Bellemare his queen. Though he cares for her, he can never say it. To do so would make his position as ruler vulnerable.

Queen Juliana of the Unblessed

From the mortal noble family of Bellemare, Juliana always dreamed of magic. But, until Merrick kidnapped her, she never realized it truly existed. Now, as Queen of Necessary Evil, she is trying to cope with the fact her new powers are derived from the misery of others.

Lord Kalen, Unblessed Noble

Dark elfin lord cursed with psychic abilities. He is empathic and clairvoyant. Leader of the fearsome Berserks, an elite unblessed army, he'd rather bury his sword than feel the emotions of others. Often driven by the need to feel nothing at all, he prefers the cold-hearted in his bed.

King Lucien of the Damned

High King of the Kingdom of Hades, Demon Ruler of Pure Evil. Living in the Fire Palace, he enjoys watching the suffering of others whether immortal or mortal. He is always plotting his evil deeds and has the patience to see them come to life. The only one who can shake his control is the nymph, Mia, who he keeps as his lover and slave—though he would never let her know that. To punish her, he currently has Mia locked in the bowels of his palace, looked after by the child soothsayer, Anja, who is pure evil.

Mia

A nymph who traded her soul to King Lucien, only to discover too late that he allowed her to keep half of it so she could still feel emotions and pleasure. But with her half-soul comes a misery and suffering she cannot escape. Lucien keeps her locked, and often chained, in his palace home. She is now the Damned King's mistress, fighting to do good where she can though darkness is pulling her into its depths.

King Ean of the Blessed

High King of the Kingdom of Tegwen, Ruler of all that is Good. Brother to Merrick, Ean lives in the Silver Palace. He is the youngest of four princes and only came to rule after the oldest, Merrick, took the Unblessed throne and the two others—Ladon and Wolfe—were presumed dead. It was learned Ladon and Wolfe were merely prisoners to the Damned King and though Ladon is free, Ean is obsessed with freeing Wolfe. He does not know what will come of his rule once his older brothers are recovered from their ordeal.

Prince Ladon of the Blessed

Brother to Merrick and Ean who spent nearly fifty years in the Damned King's prison until rescued by William the Wizard. Currently disguised by magic as the Earl of Bellemare living in the Mortal Realm.

Prince Wolfe of the Blessed

Brother to Merrick and Ean who spent nearly fifty years in the Damned King's prison, where he currently resides.

Hugh, Earl of Bellemare, faery king

Oldest of the Bellemare family, Hugh was bitten by demons known as the living dead and is unable to return to the Mortal Realm. He misses his beloved Bellemare, but can only watch it from afar. He is married to the faery queen Tania.

Tania, queen of the faeries

Lesser Queen of the faery Kingdom of Feia who lives in the Silver Palace. Flighty and often innocent to the true horrors of life and death, being as she is immortal, she doesn't always grasp what is happening.

Sir Thomas of Bellemare

Mortal brother still living at Bellemare, helping Prince Ladon stay disguised as his brother the Earl. The playful nature of the knight who could charm any lady to his bed is slowly fading into an unhappy, troubled man weighed by responsibility.

William the Wizard

The youngest of the Bellemare family, William is apprenticing to be a wizard. He cast a spell over himself, as all wizards do, to give himself bravery in the face of battle. Though, not sure that it took, he cast it three times. It takes a lot to get him worried, much to the frustration of his brothers.

Prologue

Black Palace of the Unblessed, Kingdom of Valdis, 1406 AD

Human by birth, immortal ruler by what the magical creatures called fate, Queen Juliana was new to the magical world she lived in. Her husband, King Merrick of the Unblessed, was the dark elfin ruler of the Kingdom of Valdis. He was one of the three High Kings of the immortal realm. Not pure evil like King Lucien of the Damned, with his demon filled Kingdom of Hades. But, nor was Merrick good like his estranged brother, King Ean of the Blessed. Ean ruled the Kingdom of Tegwen, a throne destined to be Merrick's by birthright, if not for fate's intervention giving him to the Unblessed. Juliana often wondered how different their lives would be now, had Ean been cursed and her husband named ruler of all that was light.

However, there was no use dwelling on what could not be. Merrick's kingdom, his very life, was a balance. Not blessed, not evil, he was merely a necessity. In the past, darker creatures had ruled as the Unblessed King, and their souls did not suffer as Merrick's now did. Being born a supreme being of the blessed, he knew what it was like to be filled with goodness and light. Now, he drew his powers from the necessary evils of the world. He was fall, winter, death to the land. When he walked through the Immortal Realm, his presence sucked the life from the world around him. Flowers wilted, grasses died, the air became cold and the sun was hidden in silver moonlight.

Because Merrick was necessary, and yet tainted by that very necessity, he existed on a small ledge between good and evil—between aligning himself with Tegwen and joining Hades, between the blessed and the damned. Juliana knew all this when she made the decision to stay eternally by his side. She became his balance, what made his reign bearable. And with her, Merrick became as good as any Unblessed King could be.

Queen Juliana chose her husband out of love because she understood how important he was. Without him, there was no good, no happiness or joy. He was as essential as light and spring. And Juliana stood by her choice, even as her magical abilities grew, as the flowers started to wilt before her, as moonlight replaced the sun, as she felt death and cold in the very power that gave her life.

A great power it was, fed by the war between the blessed and unblessed that started with her coming to the Immortal Realm. Not only a war between kingdoms, it was a war fought between the two brothers—Merrick and Ean. Surprisingly, King Lucien stayed in his Fire Palace, not involving himself, for one war suited his nature as well as any other and he enjoyed watching two brothers fight. Though Juliana was not the true cause of war, the fact that Merrick had kidnapped her was excuse enough for the two kings to raise arms. She had been a blessed ward of King Ean at the time.

At first, Merrick explained to her that war was just as necessary as peace. Unlike mortal struggles fought to free the enslaved, to protect the borders of a home or other such noble causes, the war now raging through the Immortal Realm was ultimately started because of one reason. It was deemed necessary, a cycle of life. Peace had its turn and now so should war. And, hate it as she did, she told herself she would dream of a day when peace could again have its turn. If she just waited patiently, the war would end.

That was before her power grew, before she felt each death the war brought as sure as her own heartbeat. Like her husband's existence, her body began to feed on the destruction of earth, the bitter cold that balanced the warm light of the blessed. When she married her husband, she took his burden upon herself, knowing in her heart he was never meant to bear the yoke of his reign alone.

But how could she know the full truth of such responsibility? It ran much deeper than merely ruling a kingdom of goblins, trolls, dark elves and other unblessed creatures. It was more than the mischief of the tommyknockers leading miners astray, of naughty leprechauns spreading bad luck, of the occasional blizzard that ruined crops and made food scarce. She'd inherited the unblessed darkness, the infected power that ran through her husband's blood, as much a part of him as his long blond hair or his possessive brown-black eyes. His power gave her power and the magic was linked to the very breath of their lives. They were joined eternally and each day she felt the depressive weight pulling her into its inky depths.

Without him, the immortal world would not rest. Without him, good would not be. She knew this when she married him, but she did not understand, not really. How could she? Juliana was born into the blessed mortal family of Bellemare, a noble family inherent of all that was good and pure in the human world and who shamelessly showed their love and affection. Merrick could not even say the three simple words, *I love you*. To do so weakened his powers and in turn weakened her and the unborn child she carried. So he kept his heart hidden from all, except when they were alone. Then she could see it in his expression, feel it in his touch, but it was never said.

Like a dream echoing from the past, the naive words she had said, when she decided to stay with him forever, filtered through her mind.

So long as we have each other, we will be fine. No burden is too great. Together we can get through anything. I love you. Nothing can change that.

And he had answered her with a trace of melancholy in his tone, *May you always feel that way.*

Had Merrick known even then, as he brought her into his fold, that she would waver in her determination? Could he have guessed it would be only a few short months, not even the beginning years of an eternity? It was possible he understood, for he'd once been blessed just as she was, more so as heir to the Tegwen throne, destined to become King of the Blessed. Goodness and happiness would have been his domain. But his destiny changed, and all that was blessed had become a distant memory. In time, it would be the same for her and it terrified her. She didn't want to forget what it felt like to be blessed.

Yet, considering it all, she loved him still.

Chapter One

"Why did you fight the old king?" Juliana stroked the long length of Merrick's hair from his forehead as he knelt before her. Behind her, the tapestries along the black stone walls fluttered with her question, changing from crimson to black. She felt the change, but did not see it. They were alone in their bedchamber and none of their subjects would dare enter unless summonsed. In the fireplace, the orange flames dimmed, turning blue.

Everything in the Black Palace was connected to them, magically changing with their moods. Sometimes decorating became a small power struggle, but the castle bent to the will of whoever felt stronger emotions. Then again, Juliana was sure Merrick sometimes just let her have her way. According to him, the castle wasn't built, but simply was because he was, changing and shifting as soon as he ascended the throne, replacing the old king's palace.

Merrick's hands lay on her swollen stomach and she felt tingling beneath the warm, steady palms. The sensation was more than just heat radiating from his body. Right now, his magic was inside her, his mind focused on the unborn child she carried as if holding it.

"Why did you fight the old Unblessed King?" she repeated, though she knew he'd heard her the first time.

"Is that what you're thinking so heavily about? My coronation?" She easily heard the gentle tone of his voice in the quiet bedchamber. He didn't move, didn't open his eyes. "I told you about that."

"I know it was a long time ago. You told me by killing the old king you took his place. I know the how of it, but you never said why you fought him." She touched his cheek, turning his face up so she could look into his brown-black eyes as they opened. His concentration on her stomach slipped and the tingling lessened. Leather strands wound over his hair, weaving down the length from his temples to just above his waist and she traced the coiling absently with her gaze. Juliana didn't know why she asked him, when she'd never pushed for an answer before. Somehow, today of all days, it seemed important that she understand. "If there must always be an Unblessed King, why bother killing one only to replace him? Were you tricked? Did he do something to you? Was it an accident?"

"Accident?" he whispered. She felt his slight amusement at the very thought. "How can one accidentally kill a king? It's a difficult feat."

For a moment Merrick didn't move, as he studied her face. Though he was a light elf by birth, he adopted the dark elves' manner of dress. Snug black breeches hugged his calves, hidden beneath the high boots that laced up the sides. His ash gray undertunic molded to him like a second skin, the collar upturned. Over it, he wore a sleeveless black tunic threaded with fine silver embroidery, the pattern an ancient, beautiful language. Delicate chains held the front together. The links were tiny dragons teeth to tail, with a larger dragon medallion in the middle.

When she first came, he tried to give her the more provocative outfits to match his own, but she wasn't comfortable in tight clothes that exposed more flesh than they hid—at least out of their bedchamber. As she thought of it, the high-waisted, conservative gown she wore melted. The burgundy faded to black, growing tight as the square neckline moved down to expose cleavage, even as the bodice tightened and pushed her breasts up. The material of her full skirt ripped along the side, hugging her pregnant belly.

An inner light gleamed in his eyes. "You use seduction to make me speak?"

Juliana gave him a slow smile. Her heart skipped erratically, thumping hard in her chest. He'd always had such an effect on her. From the very beginning, when she wrongly thought he killed everything she held dear, she couldn't resist him.

"Your power grows. I see it in your darkening eyes." He hummed lightly in thought. "The blue in them looks as stunning as the darkest night sky."

"I sometimes do not recognize myself." Juliana turned toward their bedchamber mirror. The tall piece of polished metal was clearer than anything she'd seen in the Mortal Realm. The elfin gown, the dark kohl lining her eyes, the winding markings drawn around her right arm from wrist to shoulder, they were all still foreign to her. But it was more than just her clothing, her eyes had darkened, as had her long brown locks. Over the months, they'd lost some of their sunburned highlights.

"It was my battle to wage as the heir to the blessed throne. The old Unblessed King embraced the death his reign brought, so much that he joined with King Lucien. Together, they enslaved wizards, hags, crones, anyone powerful they could find." Merrick again closed his eyes, nuzzling his face against her. "I don't wish to talk about this in front of my son."

Juliana laughed. Everyone was convinced the child was a boy. Perhaps they were right. According to the nature of who Merrick was, the child shouldn't have been conceived. But Juliana had learned that things were never what they seemed in the Immortal Realm.

"He rests now," Juliana assured him. "Please tell me."

"Lose the clothes first." Merrick let his power surge over her, willing her clothing to drip off her body in a warm liquid puddle around her feet. She resisted, keeping them on. "Your powers *are* stronger."

"Lord Kalen visits. There is no time for that." She patted his head, stroking back his hair.

"Let him wait."

She chuckled. "Will his Berserks be with him?"

"Nay, they stay on the battlefront. Ean hides his camp, but our wizards think they may have found where it is hidden. I've asked Kalen here alone so that he may read the baby."

Juliana forced a smile, one she didn't fully feel. "Has a fortnight passed so quickly?"

"Do not sulk, my queen. I only wish to know my son and my wife are safe." Merrick stood, a fluid, graceful movement. His dark eyes studied her and she found herself wrapping her arms around his neck to hide her face. "I do not know what would happen to me if something were to happen to you."

"I love you, too," she mouthed, only to continue aloud. "But, such things cannot be made certain. You are here and in this moment, I am safe." She felt his hands move around her back, even as the beginning press of his arousal nudged her. The length of his body was familiar and comforting. She loved being in his arms, took comfort in the smell of him as she turned her face up toward his jaw. The length of his hair dug into her shoulder, but she didn't care. "Unless there is something you keep from me?"

Juliana suspected there was. His concern over her went deeper than the normal worries of a man for his wife and child. She knew he feared his presence would suck the life from her, from their baby, but the only way that could happen was if she feared him. Juliana wasn't afraid. Not of Merrick, anyway. All other fears she buried deep, resisting their pull, refusing to give in to them.

When he didn't answer, she said, "Tell me the rest of the story of why you fought the old king."

"Together with Lucien, he conjured darkness and disease. It spread over the realm until even Tegwen lost its light. First, the trees and plants choked as if burnt by the very air. Then, the immortal creatures began to sicken and die, their flesh turning black in a way that was no longer magical, in a way that should not have been. Their flesh rotted, giant sores and swellings, puss. The illness spread so fast the sick died within days of falling victim to it."

"Plague," Juliana whispered.

"Aye, they called it the black death because the darkest magic brought it forth. The illness that had ripped through our realm leaked into the mortal one before we even knew what was happening. The old Unblessed King, knowing himself to be nearly invincible, tied the plague to his blood. When I killed him, the root of the illness ended, but it lingered in the mortal world for some time. It might linger still."

Juliana didn't answer. She'd heard men of God preach about the plague, warning it would come back to punish sinners as it had before. Whole families had been wiped out and hysteria had ruled the land. Some even said that half the world died in those long, diseased years. If the plague hadn't ended when it had, there would've been no one left in the Mortal Realm.

"You understand the why now?"

She nodded. "Aye, I understand."

"What is it? Why are you still sad?"

"You gave your blessing to save many. It seems to me that such an act should be rewarded, not punished with a life of mischief and war."

"Aye," he nodded, pulling her away from him. Looking deep into her eyes, he whispered. "Methinks I have been rewarded greatly. For fate has given me you." His hand once more slid to her stomach. "And our son. I care not what happens outside this palace, so long as you are with me."

Pain tried to roll through her heart, but she suppressed it. She couldn't let Merrick feel it. "You gave up your blessing for many. I gave mine up for you. Whatever happens, know I would not change my decision to be your queen. I love you, my king."

"And I you, sweet Juliana." He nudged her chin, trying to get her to smile. "Come to the hall with me. Let Lord Kalen read you. His presence always seems to amuse you. Or I can order Iago to set himself on fire again."

Juliana almost felt sorry for the goblin, until she remembered how he had tried to set her aflame one eve after she told them a tale that did not end to the goblin's liking. She pressed her lips to his, wanting to hold him forever, but knew he'd be suspicious if she didn't let him go. "I'll come in a moment. I want to write to my brothers. The trolls keep eating the missives I send them. Halton and Gorman have agreed to go this time."

"I could always make it easier and deliver it myself."

"Nay, they would not trust you." She gave a soft laugh. "Go, Lord Kalen arrives at the gate. Greet him and make him welcome. In fact, make him drink, for he is less surly when into his cups."

"You would be ill-humored too, if you saw the things he sees."

Juliana didn't answer. He left her, moving with infinite grace and refinement. His touch left her weak, but the absence of it unsettled her calm. Merrick opened the door, stepped out and disappeared. All the doors in the palace were like that. For anyone else, they were simply doors, but for the king and queen they took them wherever they wished to be within the castle walls. All they had to do was want to go somewhere and the castle granted the desire. Juliana concentrated, sending out her senses until she detected her husband entering the great hall.

The only place Juliana couldn't reach in the castle was the dungeons, though she knew her husband could go there whenever he wished. She shivered, looking down. The prisons were far from where she stood. It wasn't as if she wanted to go there. She felt the evil lurking behind barred doors, locked away for all eternity. Merrick had warned her once about rearranging anything in that part of the castle with her will—not that she'd been able to if she wanted to. At least, not until today. Merrick wasn't wrong when he said her power grew stronger and each time he touched the baby, her magic intensified.

Today, her will was stronger than that of her king's. The desperation she felt, the almost trapped, sinking, devilish need to end the suffering of her reign terrified her. It had only been a few months by human measurements and already her determination wavered. How had Merrick lasted nearly half a century as ruler?

"Halton, Gorman," she said when she was alone, willing the two playful sprights to come to her. They heard her call and, as always, were right there, ready to do her bidding. Aside from their tiny stature and a slight point to their ears, the two looked like human males in bright green tunics and the miniature golden crowns they insisted on wearing to show their place as the Unblessed Queen's sprights. "Do you have the message vial I made for my brothers?"

She felt bad lying to Merrick about staying behind to create a message that was already done, but she needed to buy herself some time alone. Her husband would know when the sprights left the palace, but she could only hope the notion wouldn't really take hold in his mind until it was too late for him stop her other plans.

"I have it," Halton announced, his voice ten times bigger than his body. He poked a hand into his pocket, digging around.

"Nay, I have it!" Gorman did the same.

"Do not!" Halton jerked fervently as he dug around faster.

"Do so," Gorman shouted, running his hands over his messy brown hair and knocking over his crown. "Ah, see what you made me do!"

"Ah, ha! See, here, the vial. I did have it!" Halton clutched the bright blue liquid to show her.

"Only because you stole it from me," Gorman grumped.

"My lord sprights," Juliana said, desperate to get their attention. She knelt, knowing that the inevitable fight between the two creatures was about to start. They'd literally turned arguing into an art form.

"Ah, you see that, she made me a lord because I have the vial!" Halton boasted.

"She was looking at me when she said it!" Gorman made a dive toward his friend. Juliana leaned forward, her face more on their level as she blocked the attack with her outstretched arm.

"Was not!"

"Was so!"

"No one will be a lord unless you do what I've asked of you." She kept her tone soft. They both looked up at her, their lashes fluttering over their wide blue eyes. An innocent light shone from the depths. "Please, do not argue, not now."

"What is happening?" Gorman asked.

"You seem upset," Halton continued.

"My queen, if you are frightened, know we will fight for you." Gorman took a step toward her, as if to touch her cheek.

"To the death, I'll fight." Halton pushed Gorman out of the way so he could be the first to touch her.

Juliana sat back. "I need you to get my missive to the Bellemare spright."

"Rees?" Halton and Gorman said in unison.

"Aye, Rees. Make sure he understands that he must keep it safe until he can give it to the earl in private."

"We know our mission, my lady queen," Halton bowed.

"We shall not sleep until..." Not to be outdone, Gorman did the same, continuing with a flowery speech about how he'd lay his life down for hers in combat should anything try to take the vial from him.

"Thank you." Juliana didn't wait for him to finish as she stood. "Now go. Godspeed."

"Godspeed? What does that mean?" Halton whispered as the two of them followed her to the door.

When she opened it, she willed the secret entrance leading toward the mountains near the palace to be on the other side. Though the two sprights were annoying, Juliana trusted them to perform this simple task. They might bluster and boast, but she had no doubt they'd expend their last breath to deliver her message to her brothers in the Mortal Realm.

"Methinks Godspeed means we'll be gods if we do this quickly," Gorman motioned for quiet, though his harsh whisper hardly indicated the need for discretion.

"I might," Halton snorted, "but you're way too short to be a god."

"Ho! I'm as tall as you."

"Are not!"

"Are so!"

"Just get the message to my brothers," she whispered, as the two men disappeared. The baby kicked her hard and her stomach tightened in response, contracting slightly. Rubbing the ache, she took a deep breath. "And get it there safely."

⋘⋙

Merrick felt Lord Kalen enter his hall before he saw him. The orange glow of torches mixed with that of the five large fireplaces along one of the walls. They always burned, the flames never needing attendance like those in the mortal realm. Soft light illuminated the ribbed vaults along the ceiling and danced over the towering Corinthian columns.

His goblins merrily danced, their withered bodies jerking crazily as they hopped back and forth from one foot to the other. Their short arms pumped up and down over their heads. A hairy figure, too short to be a child, too human in form to be an animal, lifted his taloned feet, clacking them against the stone floor in time to the music. A dark, wrinkled creature hung on the jutted edge of the fireplace. White hair sprouted from his head and his nose hung low over his thick, wide lips. When he smiled, he had sharp, pointed teeth. The music Merrick played for them was dark and sinister, like the underlying wind howling through ancient caves combined with the primitive drumming of sticks banging on stones. Goblin music.

Volos, the castle troll, sat in the middle of them, clapping his hands with the usual expression of idiocy on his large features. Trolls had the appearance of oversized goblins and normally lived a solitary existence. Volos was different. He was like a child, listening only to the commands of the oldest goblin, Bevil. At night, if the old goblin left him, Merrick could hear Volos whimpering in fear until Bevil came back.

As Lord Kalen entered, the man paused near the goblins, throwing up his arms and dancing in a circle with them. The elfin noble looked little more than a barbarian with a pelt of animal skin draped over his shoulder. A gold disc brooch, etched with the symbol of Kalen's ancient line, held the skin into place. He might look the part, but there was more to him than muscle and barbaric tendencies. Kalen had the burden of magical gifts.

The goblins cackled in pleasure. Kalen smiled, his purple eyes flashing as he stopped dancing only to continue on toward Merrick's throne. With him came the scent of the forest, a subtle stirring to the castle air. Long, wavy brown hair framed his face, tangled from his ride. He carried himself well, but did not move like the gentleman he was born to be. Instead, Kalen seemed like a caged animal when indoors and Merrick knew the dark elf threw himself into exhaustive physical activity to wear his energies down. It was why he liked fighting so much.

"Lord Kalen," Merrick acknowledged.

25

"My king." Kalen bowed his head.

Merrick motioned to the side, away from Juliana's throne though it was empty. A chair grew, twisting silently up from the stone floor, and a goblet of piskie ale appeared on the arm. As he drew his fingers back, a matching goblet appeared in Merrick's hand. He took a leisurely sip of the liquor, enjoying the sweet flavor and knowing Juliana liked tasting it on his mouth when she kissed him. "How is the war?"

"Violent. Long. Bloody." Kalen's smile widened as he moved to take a seat. Generally accepted as a madman, he led the elite dark elfin warriors known as the Berserks. The noble often made what appeared to be careless decisions to those peering in from the outside, sometimes calling off his troops on the eve of a great battle they'd be sure to win. He would judge a person with one touch, turning an apparently great ally from his door and accepting an unquestionable enemy into his home. Other warriors outside his Berserks thought him reckless, but the Unblessed King knew the true secret to Kalen's genius. He was a clairvoyant, cursed with empathy. It was something he didn't tell many people. "How is the queen?"

"Guarded." Merrick took another sip. He focused his feelings briefly on his wife before drawing his attention back to his friend. "I worry."

Kalen took a long drink, finishing his ale before setting down the empty goblet. Taking a deep breath, as if bracing himself, he reached toward the king, fingers pointed up, palm out. "Tell me."

Merrick pressed his palm to Kalen's, pointing his fingers up as well. The instant they touched, a thin band of light entwined their joined hands. All information Merrick wished to impart to the man flowed between them. It was over as soon as it began. Kalen slowly lowered his hand back to his empty goblet, tilting it slightly in the king's direction. "You got something stronger than ale, my king?"

Merrick chuckled, waving his hand over it to fill the drink once more. This time with a green, potent concoction the mountain wizards produced in strange stills hidden in caves. It was vile, strong and had been known to make lesser creatures sleep for days after a single sip. Kalen glanced at it, made a small noise of appreciation and took a drink without hesitation.

"Do you see why I worry?" Merrick asked, keeping to his ale.

"All carrying women have moods," Kalen answered, moving the goblet from his mouth only long enough to answer. "It passes with the birth."

"I fear it is more than that. I want you to read her just to make sure."

"So you told me." Kalen lifted the hand he'd touched to Merrick's and wiggled his fingers. "But as I've warned you before, to know the future is to know madness."

Kalen's visions were only pieces of the future—bigger pieces than most, but pieces nonetheless. When Merrick first found out about his son, he'd gone to a divining basin to see the future. The images it showed were of his hands covered in blood as Juliana screamed, her pale cheeks stained with tears. The memory of it haunted him still.

"See, madness," the noble whispered.

"Kalen, Juliana is my..." He took a deep breath, not daring to say the words out loud. To do so, to admit the depth of what he carried inside would be to weaken himself to those unscrupulous creatures who would gladly relieve him of his throne. Now was not a time to be weak. Fate had been cruel to him once when it made him decide between a life of happiness on the Blessed throne and the life he now led. Though, it wasn't much of a choice. If the old king hadn't been stopped, the Blessed throne wouldn't have been much. Would fate be cruel again? Would it take the dream of a family away from him? If he whispered how he felt about his wife, would fate hear him?

"I will read her again," Kalen said. "But, methinks it best if—"

Merrick shot to his feet. A searing pain ripped through him, a cold, barren gash in his power. He felt a burning across his gaze, indicating the whites of his eyes filled with black as he looked up to his bedchamber, every sense on alert. Bitter, icy emptiness greeted him where Juliana's essence should've been.

"What?" Kalen stood, his body tense. "What has happened?"

"Juliana," Merrick whispered, shaken. He'd sensed her great need before all traces of her disappeared completely. Panicked, his body turned to mist, drifting faster than he could run through the great hall to the door behind his throne. Going under it, he arrived in his bedchamber only to solidify. His wife was there, waiting, only she wasn't as she should be. Her body was cast in black stone, frozen in time.

"Juliana, nay. What have you done?" Merrick's heart pounded, a painful slam against the inside of his chest. He swallowed against the agony of it, as he stared at her face, willing her to break free from the stone and come to him.

One of her hands reached out as if to hold something and the other cradled the stomach rounded with their unborn child. He trembled, moving to touch her immobile face. The lingering scent of unblessed power floated in the air around him, as palpable as his own flesh. Though he searched, he could detect no other magic in the chamber. The door flung open behind him, the thick oak hitting the stone wall.

"My king?" Kalen demanded, his tone gruff with tension. "What has happened? Who has been here? Do you sense them?" He reached for his waist, pulling out a wickedly sharp dagger. Merrick smelled old blood on the blade, though it looked clean.

"She did this to herself." Merrick trembled. As he touched Juliana, the warm stone seemed to move beneath his hand with life, her life. And yet, he could see her statuesque beauty with his own eyes. She was gone. She'd left him. His heart squeezed in his chest, nearly choking him with its pain. "She imprisoned herself in stone. Only unblessed magic is... There is no other. She did this to herself."

Merrick felt the nobleman walk around them, saw him from the corner of his eyes as a blur. Kalen searched the chamber, but it was empty. Merrick couldn't take his gaze off Juliana's hard, black face. Every detail was there, the small crease in her full lips, her long eyelashes, the strands of her wavy hair resting over her ears.

Finally, Kalen stopped looking and didn't move as he stared at the queen. Merrick glared at him, demanding, "Did you foresee this? Did you know something was going to happen to her?"

"Nay, my ki—"

"Did you know?" The Unblessed King's voice lifted, rumbling as he surged toward his friend. He grabbed Kalen by the pelt and jerked him violently, dragging him toward Juliana's stone form. "You have read her. You see these things, I know you do. Why has this happened? Why did she do this? How do I free her?"

Kalen looked unconcerned by his king's anger and did not fight back. "If she did this, are you sure she'll want to be free? If only her magic is in the chamber, she must have had reason."

<![CDATA[]]>

Merrick glanced down at her pregnant stomach, feeling sick. A reason? What other reason could there be? He turned his attention to the nobleman once more, needing to lash out. "Then you did know!" Merrick lifted Kalen off the ground only to lower him back down and let go as he realized beating his friend would solve nothing.

"Nay. This I did not see. It must have been planned after I met with her last. Or else she didn't know it herself." Kalen touched the queen's outstretched hand. He closed his eyes. "I can't find her in the stone. It's like reading the wall. Are you sure you sense no other magic? To cast such a spell takes great power."

"There is only our magic in this chamber." Merrick pushed Kalen away from his wife, replacing the man's hand with his own. "Her powers were growing daily. I felt it. Mayhap she could not control this."

"You know as well as I that an act like this would take great concentration and skill. If her magic had been uncontrollable, most likely she would have blown up half the castle, not made herself a part of it."

"She's not a part of it. I would feel it if she'd made herself part of the palace. Instead, I feel nothing of her in this statue."

"Kidnapped?"

"Nay, I would have felt her leave. It's just as if she..." The king breathed hard, moving aimlessly as he searched for a sign, anything that would explain why his wife had cast herself into stone.

"She is not dead," Kalen said, though Merrick could tell by the look on his face he had no way of knowing that for sure. "We must have faith that she is safely buried within this statue waiting for the right spell to free her once more."

"I should have called you here sooner. I knew her powers were growing. Mayhap she could not control them. Mayhap we are wrong to think uncontrolled powers merely cause explosions." Merrick tried to will her from the stone, as he willed the castle to move. It didn't work. "If there was a reason, she would have left me a message. She would not leave me, not like this, not alone. She promised..."

Merrick stopped once more before his wife. Kalen touched her again, laying both hands on her. He shook his head in denial, signifying he felt nothing of her.

"No one can know of this. She's too vulnerable. I must hide her. I cannot let the vision I saw in the basin come true. I will not have her blood on my hands." He would never harm Juliana and he refused to let anyone else. "The statue must be protected."

"The Black Garden," Kalen said. "She'll be safe there. No one but you will be able to touch her. Take her to the center of the garden until we can discover a way to free her."

"Leave us, Kalen," Merrick ordered. "Tell no one of my queen. Seek out powerful wizards, whoever you have to. Read them. Find an end to this. I cannot lose her. Not now. I need her."

It was the closest he'd ever come to saying his feelings for her out loud to another person. Kalen obeyed, leaving him alone with his frozen wife in the bedchamber.

"Juliana, fate cannot take you from me now. I only just found you," Merrick whispered, knowing by the magic around him that her state was not easily undone. "You promised to stay with me."

Chapter Two

Two years later...

Tegwen Army Encampment, Mystic Forest, Immortal Realm 1408 AD

Five more dead. The victims of the war piled upon King Ean's blessed soul as the news of each death came back to the encampment. Some were friends from childhood, others elfin soldiers he'd known his whole life. For over two years he fought his brother's armies, never fully understanding why Merrick shot the first arrow of war. Did the Unblessed King truly hate him for taking what was his? Ean didn't have a choice. Merrick, the oldest, couldn't rule both kingdoms and the other two brothers, Ladon and Wolfe, were lost to them. Ean had been the only brother left who could take the responsibility. He did so without complaint, though deep inside he understood that the throne should have never been his. He hadn't wanted it.

Until Juliana's brother, William the Wizard, found the two lost princes in King Lucien's prison, they thought them dead. Now Wolfe was still trapped in the Fire Palace and Ladon lived as a mortal, disguised as an earl, taking the place of another of Juliana's brothers—the new faery king, Hugh of Bellemare. A third brother, Sir Thomas, was with Ladon in the Mortal Realm.

The Blessed King had seen Merrick on the field of battle, but naught was said about finding peace. When they were simply blessed brothers, they carried a deep connection, an understanding that only brothers could know. But when Merrick became unblessed and they'd lost Ladon and Wolfe, all that changed. Though still connected, the bond was strained.

When Merrick kidnapped one of Ean's blessed wards from the Mortal Realm, Lady Juliana of Bellemare, the act was thought to be one of war. However, Merrick surprised them all and made the woman his queen. For a time, right after, there had been a calmness to the lingering connection between them. The normal melancholy left the Unblessed King, giving Ean reason to hope that someday his brother might come back to him.

Then, on no particularly special day, the connection changed once more, becoming worse than it had ever been. Ean worried for Merrick, wondering what could have caused such a sudden shift in him. Hugh had told him about Juliana's stone prison, claiming the Unblessed King had her locked away in his garden, forever unchanging. Hugh suspected Merrick had a hand in Juliana's state. Could it be the man was right? Ean had to admit he wondered himself. Was Juliana's prison due to the child, a child who should have never been conceived? For Merrick, by the very nature of being unblessed, should not have been given a blessing so great as a child. By all accounts the child she carried was Merrick's. Since her pregnancy was an impossibility, he guessed that fate found a way to stop what should not be. Did the child and mother die, leaving a statue in their stead? Did Merrick punish Juliana? In truth, Ean had no way of knowing. No one had news of Juliana or her baby—not even the mystics.

Only a few from his camp knew the secret of the Unblessed Queen's state. Hugh only told Ean because the man had hoped the blessed could help. Ean had looked into it, but the truth was he needed to focus most of his energies into finding a way to free Wolfe from his imprisonment. He did not know Juliana, only of her, and had no real reason to see the Unblessed Queen free without knowing why she was trapped in the first place. It wasn't as if Merrick asked for his help in the matter.

"Why, Merrick?" Ean mumbled, thinking again of the war.

"My king?" Commander Adal stopped in his approach, giving him a questioning glance. He wore the red tunic of the Tegwen guards. It hung down over his legs, parting in the front. As head of the light elfin guard, answering only to King Ean, he'd proven himself a capable leader.

"Settling things in my mind," Ean said. "It's naught."

"We should move the encampment." Commander Adal did not question the king. "Word came from King Hugh that the faeries detected a patch of dead forest near here. They work to fix it, but he worries Merrick's men come too close."

"Even as a mortal he couldn't seem to stay out of our affairs," Ean mused. "Now as a faery, methinks he longs for a reason to be called to join us."

"Faeries have their place in the war and it is not in battle, but in our beds, lifting our spirits and fueling our energy." Adal chuckled at the thought. Many of the faeries came to the encampment. Power and magic could be made from such things as passion and pleasure. "And important role that is, too."

"I'm sure that is a role King Hugh would not wish to play."

"And the happier I am for it," Adal jested. "I don't favor men in my bed."

"Methinks it cannot be easy going from mortal warrior to faery," Ean said.

"I suppose you're right, but regardless he's a faery by his own choice."

Sunlight glowed over the encampment, falling in streams from amongst the tree branches overhead. Nearby a clearing covered with tiny blue flowers grew, leading in a trail over the floor as if following the steps of faery feet. Undoubtedly, the faery women who'd been at the camp the night before had left the flowers. Sweet perfume carried on the afternoon breeze, making Ean forget for a moment that he did not wish to be there. Tents jutted from the ground, a haphazard pattern like the growing of trees, connected only by the light patches of earth worn into paths.

"Strange that he takes up our cause when Merrick is married to his sister," Adal said. "Though I sent men to the forest to check and he tells the truth about the worn grass."

"There is no mystery. Hugh still believes we can save Juliana from Merrick. He does not like the Unblessed King." Hearing a neigh, Ean glanced to where a few of his unicorn mounts grazed. Their majestic bodies rippled with muscles as they walked, the velvet of their coats gleaming with the waving patterns of light. "He blames Merrick for her stone prison."

"A mystery, to be sure."

"Aye, one we will not solve. Thankfully, it's not our mystery." Ean glanced at him. "You didn't come to speak of my brother's wife. What is it?"

"Have you heard?" Adal asked, his mood instantly darkening. "Five more in last eve's skirmish."

"Aye, just this hour past." Placing his hands on his hips, Ean looked up at the sky, taking a deep breath. The perfumed air no longer gave any pleasure, nor did the perfect breeze he had the wizard maintain over the encampment beneath the protective shield conjured to hide their location. "Flannan of the Green, the brothers Aubert and Bardolph, Yves the Archer and Griffen of the North Valley. Their families will have to be told."

"Ivon awaits your missives and will ride as soon as you're ready."

Ean reached into the neck of his long tunic. Maroon embroidery accented the white cream-colored material. Falling to just below his knees, a matching pair of breeches hung loose about his legs. A crown wrapped his forehead, the gold dipping down in front before disappearing beneath the locks of his long blond hair. Pulling out four letters bound with ribbon, he handed them to Adal. "Already done."

Adal took them, holding them to his side as he continued talking. "Onfroi arrived. I directed him to your tent."

Ean glanced instantly toward the center of the camp. "I must speak with him at once. He comes with news from outside the Fire Palace."

"That's the fifth wizard you sent to test the palace's defenses," Adal said, looking almost instantly sorry for his hasty observation.

"And I will send a thousand more if it means freeing my brother. I will find a way into the palace. I have to. It's not as if Lucien will just let Wolfe go now that we know he's alive." Irritated, Ean marched off. He understood the commander's first concern was for the war, but the king could not give up on his brother. Over fifty years had been wasted not realizing the man was there. Now he knew Prince Wolfe was alive and he'd find a way to save him.

Black Palace of the Unblessed, Kingdom of Valdis

"Fly away, boy, naught has changed since your last visit here." Merrick didn't bother to look up from where he lounged over the arms of his throne. Juliana's place beside him was gone, her seat banished into the castle floor so as not to remind him that his wife could not sit in it.

"I've brought another potion to try." King Hugh did not pause in his stride as he moved across the stone. Merrick already knew the man had brought something. Juliana's brother always brought a potion or a spell each time he came. The man had exhausted nearly all the faery magic and still did not give up his quest to free his sister.

Merrick, in the darker hours of his discontentment, tried to convince himself not to care about his stone queen, but the words were always a lie. Just like Hugh, he could never relinquish the hope of his Juliana. The Unblessed King supposed that is why he sent his goblins away and why he allowed Hugh back into his castle, even as he had the power to bar the faery king from ever entering.

"And a spell." Though he had wings, Hugh did not clothe himself like the rest of the male faery. Perhaps because he was born human, he did not wear the shimmering cloth or the sparkling sheen of the others. Instead, he wore the clothes of the human male—a brown long tunic that fell to his knees, dagged hemlines, a high-standing collar and wide shoulders. However, unlike the human style, his boots were tall and made from hard material, better for protecting his feet. "Shall we argue again, Merrick, or will you spare us both the fight and lead me into the Black Garden to see her."

Merrick sat quietly for a long moment, knowing all along he'd lead Hugh to the garden, knowing he'd hope with every ounce of his magic while the faery tried to free her, knowing that in the end his heart would break in their failure. If he could avoid going, he would, but only he could cross to the garden in the center of the thorn labyrinth. Any other who tried would get lost and eventually die.

"Well?"

"What questionable creature did you get this spell from?" Finally, Merrick stood, not bothering to motion Hugh to follow as he walked to the door behind his throne. Hugh answered the taunting with his own.

"Have you recovered Juliana's knife from Lucien?" Hugh asked, as he always did. The jeweled weapon had been a gift to Juliana from her brothers. Lucien had kidnapped Hugh and the faery king had seen it in the Damned King's possession.

"I already told you, as I tell you each time, she probably left it on the table when she told stories to the goblins. One of them must have taken it and lost it. Lucien has not been in my home since Juliana stabbed him and I have no intention of going to the Fire Palace unless it is to free my brother Wolfe from the prisons."

The narrow hall was plain, except for the decorative arches overhead. No sound came from within as the two men walked toward a door. A small round window with the silhouetted head of a dragon was above it, marking the entrance to the Black Garden. From the pointed lancet windows in other parts of the palace, one could see the ominous landscape. The castle settled between the mountain range and the great forest.

A window looked out over the path, showing the moonlight that always shone over the garden. The shadowed black stone led to a walled courtyard. Merrick didn't pause, not needing to tell Hugh to stay close. The faery king already understood some of the dangers of the labyrinth that lay beyond the courtyard walls. They walked outside into the cool night, their way illuminated by the silver cast of moonlight. The castle loomed overhead as they walked away, the hooked spires twisting morbidly into the clear sky.

A side yard extended from both sides of the black cobblestone, but it was only a glamour, hiding the deep pit beneath the grassy surface. The two men stayed on the path, not pausing as Merrick walked straight for the arched entryway to the garden. Once through, the path veered off in several directions. Merrick continued straight, hearing the crunching footfall of stones beneath their feet as neither of them spoke.

The vine-covered walls of the garden soundlessly parted, covered in blood red flowers that nearly dripped in liquid splendor. Thorns, as sharp as blades, edged the vines, but as Merrick walked, they never touched him. Hugh stayed close as the path closed behind them. A few times he cursed, as the bladed thorns came too close to his wings. It wasn't long before they were in the center section of the garden, a stone floor stretched out, enclosed by the vines. Benches and empty vases created nooks, but neither of them moved to sit. Their attention focused on Juliana, her body captured in stone.

"She's moved again," Hugh said.

"Aye." Merrick agreed. Today his wife's statue sat on the platform, her knees drawn up as her elbows braced on them. Her face lay in her cupped hands and her expression was one of complete boredom. "More often now everyday."

"I would almost prefer it if she did not move," Hugh said "Then we could go back to looking for her kidnapper. I liked the idea of this statue being a clever ruse to put us off the scent of the hunt."

"I like knowing she's here and safe," Merrick disagreed. Though stone, at least here he could touch her—here and in his spell-cast dreams. Though unlike the dreams he gave himself of her, the stone figure was real. It just didn't touch him back.

"I worry that her movement means she's settling into her stone prison. Or maybe she's breaking free." Hugh sighed heavily, staring down at her.

Merrick didn't take the man's hope away, but Juliana wasn't breaking free. If she were, his sense of her would become stronger. It stayed the same. "What potion have you brought today?"

"Conjuring." Hugh lifted his tunic and pulled a satchel from his waist. "It's to call lost family."

"She's not dead and the things brought forth from conjuring potions are usually best left where they are. The walking dead—"

"We've tried everything else." Hugh's tone was tight.

Merrick knew from experience what came next and he didn't have the energy for it. "You asked to avoid the fight in the hall and now I ask you to return the consideration. I have no wish to hear your accusations of how this never would have happened had she been with you at Bellemare." Merrick turned his attention to the statue. Juliana's hair was frozen as if drifting in a breeze. Though he watched, sometimes for hours, he never saw her statue move, only came to see it in a different position in his garden.

"Fine," Hugh agreed. He opened a vial he carried and moved to pour the contents over his sister's stone head. Bright green trailed between the grooves that carved her features, dripping like a tear over her cheek, down her neck, sliding between her breasts. Then, unrolling a small scroll, he began to whisper.

Merrick drowned out the man's words. They sounded practiced to the point that the diction of Hugh's voice was overly pronounced. The faery king's wings didn't move and even seemed to droop in sadness.

Merrick stepped back, staring at his wife. The backs of his knees hit a stone bench and he sat, close to the thorn-covered walls, surrounded by the crimson flowers that seemed to melt with blood. They were the only flowers that bloomed around him in the immortal realm. Everything else withered and died. He couldn't help thinking that maybe it really was his fault Juliana was in stone. Perchance his presence did drain her as he did everything else. Mayhap it was their child that did it, his blood growing inside her. He had felt strength in the child.

"It did not work," Hugh said.

Merrick blinked, not having realized the man was done.

"I didn't think it would, but I had to try," Hugh said "William is coming to visit me at Feia. Actually, he was to be there before I came here, but this spell needed to be performed on this day to work so I came without him. My young brother could never keep track of time and always finds some reason for delay. I sent word for him reminding him to come, but..." He gave a humorless laugh. "He's been researching possibilities in the scrolls given to him by his wizard master. With luck, I'll be back soon to try again."

Merrick didn't move. Though he hadn't expected Hugh's efforts to work, he still felt the acute disappointment rolling through him, even as he felt his power growing from Hugh's frustration. Normally, he could ignore such a small infusion, but the man was standing too close.

"Aren't you going to tell me not to bother, as you always do?" Hugh asked, his tone dropping slightly.

"Nay." Merrick shook his head. He lifted his hand to the side, forming a cloth within his grasp. The soft, black material slid between his fingers as he stood. Going to his wife, he knelt before her. Gently, he wiped the green trails from her face left from Hugh's magic, cleaning each groove of her complexion with care and tenderness. His hands strayed to her stomach. Sometimes, when he concentrated really hard, he swore he could feel his son kick. But he was confident that it was only his imagination that caused the sensation. The stone didn't move, didn't answer his nearness or the call of his power. Was this his fate? To come to the Black Garden to watch her for eternity, moving when he couldn't see?

This is what his life had become. Hell. Though a few human years were hardly anything compared to the full course of his immortal days, it had been a very long time to wait. Merrick could still hear her laugh, see her smile, taste her kiss.

"Ah, my Juliana," he whispered, momentarily forgetting he was being watched. "Why did you not leave me a way to free you?"

"I know you love her," Hugh said. Merrick tensed, realizing he'd said the words out loud so the other could hear him. "I didn't believe it before, but when I became king, when I became a faery, I felt that love. I feel it now."

"And I feel how that knowledge pains you even more," Merrick answered, not looking at the man.

"Aye, it does, for I can't sense how my sister truly feels about you."

"So you no longer think this is my fault?"

"Nay, methinks you're greatly to blame, but I don't hate you as I once did." Hugh cleared his throat. "Do not misunderstand. I don't like you, but I don't wish you dead with every thought. I know, in your way, you love my sister. However, I still believe my sister to be bewitched by you, Merrick. Methinks that is the reason she turned her back on her blessing and her family to stay with you."

"Cease," Merrick ordered, pushing to his feet. "Speak no more of things you do not understand. At least do not speak of them to me for you will not find a willing ear."

"But—"

"If you wish me to bring you to the garden again, you will stop speaking." Merrick concentrated on controlling the shiver that racked over him. Hugh's little speech was not meant to comfort, but Merrick didn't think the faery king understood just how deep the blade of his words stabbed. Had Merrick not berated himself several times for taking Juliana from Bellemare, only to give her a fate sealed in stone? The Unblessed King dropped the cleaning rag and it disappeared before hitting the stone ground. He couldn't banter with Hugh today, not now. Without making sure Hugh followed, he walked straight toward his castle, parting the stone as if running away from Juliana could stop the pain in his heart.

Fire Palace of the Damned, Kingdom of Hades

"Delicious pain, such anguish and torment. Can you not feel it? Running through my blood. Wonderful agony." Anja danced around the barren cell hidden in the bowels of the Fire Palace, twirling and twisting her graceful arms until each perfect movement looked like curling smoke. She was a tiny thing, with deceivingly soulful blue eyes and blonde ringlet hair. A cherub, an angel, the perfect figure of innocence, all hiding the utter darkness and hate boiling beneath her pale, rose-tinted flesh.

Her voice rang like a child at play, for that is exactly what she was—an evil, malicious child in her dungeon filled with horrific toys. To entertain her bloodlust, prisoners were kept under her complete control, strapped and bound, their bodies ready for a hot poker or dull sword blade—and that was on her merciful days. Perhaps seeing innocence but feeling agony at its hands was her most effective torture device, for it served as a reminder that here in hell not even the angels would save you.

Mia awoke to Anja's dance and the almost lullaby tone of her voice as she spoke. Metal strips held Mia by her ankles and wrists, locking her limbs to the unevenly grooved grate beneath her. Chains held it on the ceiling, allowing the device to be swung around. Little specks of ash floated in the air, the dead gray reflecting the blood red firelight. Mia watched them, seeing patterns form impossible faces. The childlike voice of her captor sang to the music of screams and howls. Pleas for mercy went unheeded, often drawing more venom than it relieved. This was a place of forgetting. Not even death would come for them here. Not in Anja's care.

Kept in a deep pit, there was no escape for the forgotten who lived within the cold walls, encased in the terrifying stench of demon blood and burnt flesh. Somewhere, hidden down a corridor where Mia couldn't see, magical creatures of all races dwelled within their hellish fate. She came to know them by their cries, naming them in her head so she didn't feel so alone. Almost worse than being awake was being asleep. Dreams, if they were good, became a mocking torment. And, if they were bad, it only continued the torture of the wakeful mind.

Mia couldn't remember how long she'd been chained in the dungeon, tormented by the child's voice, held helpless with thoughts of what Anja said she wanted to do to her. But, for some reason, the child never touched her, never set the hot poker completely to the flesh though the heat from it often threatened. At first, she thought Anja's game a new kind of hell, the torment of the unknown. When would the torture start? How bad would the pain be? How could she possibly endure it?

But days became sennights, which in turn bled into fortnights, until time no longer had meaning and she remained untouched.

"Delicious pain," Anja whispered, her breath causing Mia to gasp as it fanned over her cheek. The soothsayer was close now.

The child giggled and the sound of her feet skipped around the metal rack. "Can you feel it yet, Mia? Can you taste the fear? Do you crave it yet?"

"Cease, soothsayer," she whispered. "I want to hear no more of your ramblings. Kill me or leave me be."

Mia hoped the child killed her.

"Oh!" Anja pouted. The rack moved as the soothsayer climbed onto the bottom, sitting between Mia's pinned legs. "Do not speak your mean words to me, tied one. You know not what things I see in my powerful prison. As your fear comes, so do the visions. I see you, helpless babe. You pretend not to, but you know why you're here, dark lady."

Mia gave a weak laugh. "Because Lucien is punishing me. It's not a great secret."

Anja crawled forward, her small hands pressing into her prisoner's stomach. Her blonde hair fell forward, framing her rounded features. Whispering, she pronounced each word carefully, "Not here in the dungeons, here in the palace. I know your true secret, my sweet. But don't worry, dark lady, I won't tell the Demon King."

The red fire surged and Anja turned her head quickly toward the corridor. The rack swung lightly, almost sickeningly as the child pushed up. Mia groaned, feeling her world spin.

"A new doll for me to play with!" Anja gasped in pleasure, clapping her hands. "It has been so long since the king brought me a new doll. I shall torture him at once."

The pattering of feet led the child away, leaving Mia to rest unharmed. Weakly, she pulled at her wrists, but they were bound by more than metal. Magic held her more effectively than bars ever could. She concentrated on the jagged ceiling, as she willed the rack to stop rocking.

"Mia?"

The sound was familiar, a scraping from her past that pulled at the memories in her head. She didn't move, having heard the echoes of her memory before.

"I've found you!" came a hurried whisper. The rack moved again, swinging harder as footfall rushed over the stone. It was heavier than Anja's, making deep thuds.

"William?" Mia found the strength to lift her head as she saw a figure moving in the corner of her eye. "William the Wizard? Do I see glamours?"

"We must hurry. The soothsayer and the king won't be distracted long with their new prisoner," he insisted. "And this cloak of magic I have will not keep long."

"What are you doing here?" Mia craned her neck to watch him.

"Don't you know?" William's face appeared over her, his brown hair longer than she remembered. It hung around his features. He wore the brown, plain robes of a wizard. Though such a thing by apprenticeship, he was still a mortal from the human line of Bellemare. The youngest sibling, he came from a family graced with beauty and charm. Truly blessed in many ways, they held an inner light that shone in their gaze. Mia was too tired to see that light now, as she looked into the familiar face. She supposed it was hard for anyone to hold much light in a place of such evil darkness. Or perhaps it was whatever spell the wizard used, the only way he could come undetected into the bowels of the Fire Palace. "You saved me once from this very prison. I am returning the favor. I care for you. I owe you."

"Still fearless, aren't you, wizard? You should cast a spell to reverse that which makes you so. For we both know it's by no natural means you find the strength to come in here." She laughed softly, the sound humorless. "Your face is unchanged from that man I met at Bellemare before Lucien kidnapped you.

It feels as if it should have. It feels as if I have been down here much longer, too long for you to be alive. And yet here you are, your unmarked face telling me that time has indeed been slow. Your gaze is as dark as sin, just like your brother Hugh. But you don't sin, do you, William? You, who are good and pure. You didn't deserve to be in this place any more than Hugh did."

A strange expression fell over the wizard's features. "Close your eyes. You mustn't look. The light might become too bright after so long in darkness."

What else did she have to do but obey? Closing her eyes, she waited for a jolt of power, a clank as he tried to pry the metal apart. "I should warn you. The metal is protected by magic. Only Anja and the king can open it."

"Already done," William said. "Now, come, we must hurry."

She opened her eyes to discover her limbs were free. How had he done it? Before, when she'd removed his shackles—part of the reason she found herself where she was—she'd had to use King Lucien's flesh and blood, scraped from his back during sex. "William, how did you get...?"

"There isn't time to explain," he insisted, pulling her arm. "Well, there is time. Of course there is time, but no time to continue talking. Speech is—"

"William," she interrupted.

"We will speak on it later, but first a daring escape!"

"Shh," she hushed, wishing he hadn't triple cast the spell for bravery over himself. It didn't make him invincible, only without a normal sense of fear. She was weak from her stay in the prison, but the very idea of getting out gave her strength to follow where he led. To her surprise, he passed the corridor's entryway and turned to the red fire.

"Give me your hand," he ordered. "When the king leaves and the flames surge, we jump. It's the only way out."

47

"Why do you risk this?" She didn't reach for his hand, instead staring at his clean fingers.

He gave her a weak smile and she caught a brief glimpse of love in that expression. Mia wanted to weep. She didn't deserve love.

Reaching into the front of his robe, he pulled out his wand. His hand shook, Mia's legs tensed and then the fire burned bright, surging violently. Time slowed as William tugged her hand, leaping into the flames. She expected to feel the bite of heat but instead found bitter cold. The instant white-hot pain felt as bad as fire, but was over quickly.

On the other side, they fell forward, only to hit hard upon uneven rocks. The first thing she noticed was the cool breeze, fresh and crisp over her skin. Warmth invaded her, not the choking heat of a fireplace, but the sweet caress of sunlight. Her eyes came to focus on the tall fiery pillar of Lucien's palace. They were outside the Damned King's gate. Flames engulfed the stone, a daunting sight to any who would try to enter. But Mia knew the way in, understood that she was a part of the fire because Lucien had half of her soul. She'd always be allowed in. It was walking out that was the problem. But now she was out.

"Free." Her voice cracked.

"Aye, free," William said. "Can you run? I have horses. Feia is close. I can take you to my brother Hugh and there we can—"

"I'm not going with you, William." Mia trembled as she pushed to her feet. Part of her was drawn to the palace.

"But—"

"You should not have risked yourself to free me. Consider whatever debt you feel you have, because I saved your life, to be paid in full. Now go. You should not have come here. Good and pure souls don't belong here."

"Mia, is this because you fear Lucien? I'm not scared of him. Let him give chase. I have a plan. I know what I'm—"

She backed away from him, shaking her head. "Sinners belong here, William. I belong here. I long to leave, but Lucien has my soul. With it he can find me anywhere. I am his until he lets me go."

"Nay!" He lunged for her, but Mia stumbled back, falling into the flamed wall.

Unlike escaping from the prison, the flames didn't hurt as they consumed, roaring in her ears. The hard stone floor cushioned her fall, stinging her flesh as she was once more inside the walls of the great palace. She lay in her dark corner, breathing hard as the walls seemed to loom in. "Fare thee well, freedom. I am home."

Not bothering to stand, she crawled toward a long row of twisted stairs, leading up a tower that would take her to Lucien's bedchamber. There was nowhere else for her to be. Lucien would find her and perhaps send her back down to the dungeons once he did. Until then, she'd rest on his bed and hope that he showed her mercy.

Chapter Three

Out of all the things in the immortal realm that could kill a once mortal queen, Juliana never dreamt it would be boredom that did her in. She'd been through all the emotions in her two years waiting to be rescued—surprise, fear, dread, sadness, anger, even slight madness and now boredom. Never ending, soul sucking boredom. And, though she loved her son, being kicked from the inside for so long a time was beginning to wear on her. No woman should have to be pregnant for over two years.

"Even so," Juliana said aloud to hear herself speak, "I would not change it." She patted her stomach.

The ashen stone world was dead, leaving her as one of the only things living in the realm of rock. Not even the air seemed to stir unless she disturbed it. Everything here was oddly familiar, yet different than as it should be. When the old witch from the bowels of the Black Palace agreed to help her, she neglected to tell Juliana that instead of sleeping in stone, she'd be banished to a world where everyone else was rock and she was living flesh, cursed to live alone with only the subtly changing images of the man she loved to keep her company.

The Black Palace stood, its color a pale gray and charcoal, as did the rest of the land—the forest, the mountains, even the goblins that filled her husband's hall. She had little power here and could not move about at will. Instead, she wandered the castle day after day, looking to find where Merrick's form hid. His statue haunted her, sometimes in the main hall lounging across his chair as she'd seen him do often. She would sit in her throne next to him, or sometimes on his lap, cuddling into his chest, tortured to touch his figure but not really feel him. Her heart ached and she missed him terribly. Stone was no replacement for flesh.

Other times, he'd be in bed—thankfully always alone. Juliana tried to make him feel her. She touched him, laid next to him on the hard, cold slab of his bed, but she never knew if it worked. Arousal plagued her, unfilled passions that made her body ache to be touched, made worse when Merrick slept without clothes or coverlet.

That is how she passed the first of her long days. However, as months passed and Merrick did not do what the witch was instructed to tell him to do, she stopped trying so hard. Was his war really that much more important than his wife? Had she underestimated his love for her? Had she overestimated the Blessed King wanting peace? Or was it that as an immortal, two human years felt like nothing to him and he did not think of her one way or another?

Soldiers came to the hall, sometimes filling it with their large, barbaric forms. The goblins were there—Tuki, Bevil, Iago and the rest—moving when she couldn't see. They made a field of mischievous statues, picking their noses, scratching their backsides, lighting each other on fire. Juliana had tried reaching them all, but never did they show signs of getting her message. She was truly trapped.

Then, the day came when her throne no longer stood next to Merrick's. Her husband had willed it away and it was all she could do not to throw rocks at his head in hope of breaking it off. But something else happened that day. The dark, crawling shadows, the other things that lived in the stone world, came. They were sprits, ghosts, floating and skimming along the edge of her sight. Occasionally they'd whisper, cruel taunting sounds to make her go mad.

"He forgets you, my lady."

"No longer a queen."

"He forgets your child."

"He doesn't love you. He never loved you."

"Death is the only way out of here."

"Death."

There were dark times when she almost slipped. Finding death wouldn't be hard, not with all the sharp edges of stone just waiting to be broken off and plunged into her aching heart. But to kill herself would be to kill her son. Such an act would not free her from the stone prison. Only one thing could break her spell.

Then her son would move inside her, kicking her, reminding her that she did this out of the fear of him being born into an unblessed world of war and death, one where the chance that his father might be killed at any time was much higher, leaving them helpless. She didn't want his first feelings to be the ones of people dying. Her son's power would come from the same place her husband's did. No child should be born into complete misery. Wintry death would not be her son's only bedtime story. Mischief and madness would not be his nursery song.

Juliana did the only thing she could think of to force peace. She'd summonsed a presence she felt within the dark bowels of her palace home, an old witch living in the dungeons. But the woman was not a prisoner. Her door was not locked and she carried some of Merrick's blood with her. It was only a few drops, but Juliana knew the woman's loyalty by it. Merrick would not have given it to her otherwise.

The old crone lived under the Unblessed King's protection. Together, she and the witch hatched a plan to bring the war to an end. In doing so, Juliana hoped they might mend the broken bond between Ean and Merrick. Her son had a right to know of his blessed heritage. After she became stone, something that should have been a resting place and not this strange realm, Merrick would feel her absence and discover what she'd done. The witch was to wait by her statue and give the jeweled dagger to her husband with the simple instructions he would need to free her.

Juliana ignored the awful spirits, blocking them from her mind as she found small hope in the presence of Merrick's statuesque body. When he did not free her, she began to wait for Kalen. With the man's abilities, he'd be able to hear her call if anyone could. Unfortunately, by the time she realized she needed to try, he did not appear at the palace and she knew she would have to leave her home to find him.

Every time she thought of it, she got sick to her stomach. Never did she think it would take Merrick so long to act. Was she being punished for trying to force his hand? Did Kalen read it in her future and tell him what she would do before she did it? Did he stop their spell and cast her into the stone purgatory as a punishment?

Like her un-growing belly, her body did not change. She did not need to eat, did not thirst for water. It was as if her life had stopped in a single second. Though, she did discover that she could be hurt. She'd cut her foot once while dancing barefoot in the ashen Black Garden. The wound had healed, but it was a valuable lesson. She might not be living in her rocky existence, but she could die in it.

As even more time passed, she felt a tingling pull, as if someone called to her. Then, one day, the tingling became a buzzing and she was drawn to a dream-like state, until she couldn't tell if she was awake or asleep. Merrick was there, filling the physical void. They couldn't speak, couldn't communicate, but they could touch. Almost desperately, they clung to each other, making feverish love as if the moment might end. Those rare nights in his arms became her center and she waited endlessly for them to come.

Pacing the great hall, back and forth, back and forth, desperate for something to happen, she skidded to a stop as she saw Merrick suddenly at his throne, seated behind his set table ready to dine. Angrily, Juliana stalked across the floor and placed her hands on the cool table, yelling, "Rescue us already, you dimwit!"

Rivershire, Clishmore River Bank, Neutral Territory

"Let me see the list," Gorman demanded, leaping for Halton. He knocked the spright over and struggled to grab the rolled parchment from his hand. "I allowed you to carry it here. Now, give it to me. I will represent King Merrick in these dealings."

"Allowed me?" Halton snorted derisively. "You allowed me? King Merrick gave this to me and told me to carry it here." He shook his fist, keeping the missive just out of Gorman's reach as he dug his heels into the ground to push back.

Suddenly, a large hoof swept in from the side, propelling the both of them several yards down the bank of the Clishmore River. They hit the water with a thud, still locked together in battle over the parchment. But, instead of sinking beneath the surface, they found a soft haven between the scaled, dark breasts of a mermaid. Instantly, the two sprights stopped struggling, sharing a grin as they looked up into the beautiful face of the swimming temptress.

"Ah!" The mermaid screeched, flicking the tips of her webbed fingers at them until she managed to get them off.

The two sprights landed back on shore, rolling in the mud. Gorman bit Halton's shoulder, causing him to let go of the parchment. Victorious, Gorman struggled to his feet and jumped up and down, causing clumps of mud to fly from his tunic. "I am the parchment keeper. All fall prostrate within the scope of my—*umph.*"

Halton regained his treasure as a dazed Gorman recovered from a blow across his jaw. Halton glanced up to see the large troll skulking off, unaware of the spright he just trampled.

"Why'd you have to hit me so hard?" Gorman pouted, though he didn't try to take the parchment again.

Halton again glanced at the troll, hid his smile as he took credit for the blow that was not his and balled his small hand shaking it at Gorman. "I'll do it again, too, if you're not careful."

Gorman flinched.

"Aye, methought as much." Halton puffed out his chest. Unrolling the now crumpled, wet parchment, he shook it. The ink ran, blurred almost beyond reading. "First, we need, ah, we need, um, pig mugwarp."

"Pig mugwarp?" Gorman frowned, craning his neck to read without getting too close. "What's that?"

"If you don't know, I'm not going to tell you."

"Are you sure it doesn't say big bugwanp?"

"We'll get mugwort," Halton said.

"Ah, aye, mugwort." Gorman nodded. "And marjoram."

"Why marjoram? You need a love spell?"

"It's pretty and who knows, I might need a love spell once Queen Juliana comes back and makes me a lord."

"Aye. Pretty. But she said she'd make me the lord, not you." Halton glanced up and down the bank, as if trying to decide which way to go.

"Did not!"

"Did so!" Halton growled, lifting his fist. Gorman quieted, touching his injured face. "Methinks it would just be easier if King Merrick asked us how to free our queen, instead of trying all these spells that do not work."

"Aye, but we cannot tell him anyway. We're the queen's sprights, not the king's." Gorman sniffed. "And you know these elves. They like to figure such things out for themselves. It's all sport to them."

"Aye, we are most loyal to Queen Juliana of the Unblessed," Halton's voice rose to make sure anyone listening could hear him. Both sprights puffed out their chest. His voice became louder with each word. "Besides, methinks King Merrick, our close friend, needs our help in this important matter. He sends us on these quests because we are his most trusted warriors."

"Oh, aye," Gorman agreed. "His bravest knights, to be sure."

"More feared than the Berserks!"

"Aye, and—"

A cloaked human passed, kicking his feet between them as he walked. The two sprights rolled out of the way, grumbling even as they tried to get off the main pathway leading up from the river.

Tethered boats rocked in steady thumps against the docks. Some were simple rafts, created from rough-hewn logs tied together to make platforms. Bundled reeds, lashed tight to form a hull, floated next to them. A larger, more elaborate sailboat complete with twenty-four oars towered over the others. Along its sides were the green slashed markings to indicate nobility from the sea colonies.

The two sprights skipped beside the ancient Clishmore River before finding an easy slope to hop up. The marketplace city of Rivershire stretched before them for miles. Behind them, merfolk swam along the shore. The dark temptress they'd landed on was amongst them. She frowned, pointing at the sprights. Gorman hurried further from the water.

The marketplace was special, for it was the only place in the entire immortal realm that fell under no one king's domain. It was neutral territory, often the trading place of black and white magic. Hopefuls came to find apprenticeship in wizardry and magic, blessed and unblessed alike came to trade wares and even the rare demon had been known to come through. Lord Griffen, the elected nobleman, officially controlled it all.

"A tavern." Halton pointed toward a wooden building.

"I do not think the king said anything about ale." Gorman craned his neck to see the list.

Halton snapped it away, not letting him see. "It's on there twice. Nay, three times."

"Well, then." Gorman rubbed his hands. "Then we better get to drinking!"

"Aye, to drinking," Halton agreed, shoving the parchment into his tunic.

Silver Palace of the Faeries, Kingdom of Feia

"I don't know if there is anything more we can do for them, my love." Queen Tania of the faeries frowned, eyeing the door that led to the three sick faeries—Jolynne, Nyda and Leliah. "This is an illness I have never seen."

57

"Nicholas was possessed by Lucien's demon when he took them to his bed." Hugh wrapped his arms around his wife's waist as she hovered over the floor. He preferred to keep his feet firmly on the ground, reluctantly flying only when she forced him to practice his daily lessons on his faery magic.

"I should have sensed the demon in him, but your presence distracted me so. I did not realize how much of my attention was taken away with my desire to possess you." She smiled, little dots of light coming off her wings, letting him know she wanted him—always wanted him. Taller than the other natural born faeries, her face was on level with his as she kept her feet off the floor. She was slender, with delicate white wings threaded with silver veins. The silken locks of her waist-length blonde hair surrounded her body. She kept it parted in the middle, held in place by a crown of diamonds set in silver. The sparkling stones matched the celestial material of her white gown.

"If anyone could have seen it, I would have. I have known Sir Nicholas since boyhood." Hugh frowned, again looking at the silver doors. The few times he'd seen the sick faeries had left him cold.

The doors matched the silver of the palace walls. Ancient faery symbols were etched over the length of the walls and doors, amplifying their power to hide the evil on the other side. The magical barrier kept the royal couple from feeling inside. To do so would only make them sick with the darkness that loomed over the three ill faery women.

"Nicholas..." Hugh couldn't say the words, but knew he didn't have to. The last time he'd seen the man, Nicholas had traded his soul to King Lucien. It was one of Hugh's greatest regrets. He couldn't save him.

"The man you know is no more. You couldn't do anything. He made his own choices." Tania touched his cheek. "You are a good man, my love. When it comes to Lucien, everyone makes their own choice. Nicholas bartered his soul. He must have been in great pain, too great for you to fix."

"Methought faeries did not think of such things?" He kissed the tip of her nose.

"We learn." Tania took a deep breath, looking at the door. "Whatever I felt in Lucien during my time of darkness, I feel it in there. His magic infects them and I fear I cannot save them. Methinks they are dying."

"Say the word and I will end their suffering. It may be the humane thing to do."

"Nay, that is an order it's not in me to give. I cannot give up hope."

Hugh reached for Tania's hand, holding it as he pushed the door. It opened easily and he felt his wife steel herself. Being faery born, she was delicate to such things as sickness and death. He'd been born human, only turning when he mated with Tania. As a human earl, he'd seen much battle and death. Evil might churn his stomach, but he could handle it. It was more feeling her distress that bothered him. She was his true weakness.

"They are gone!" Tania gasped, her eyes wide as she stared toward the direction of the three empty beds. They were in the middle of the circular chamber, lit by a dim light coming through the crystal ceiling. "How?"

"Look." Hugh let go of her hand and moved toward the nearest bed. Yellow-tinted faery dust covered it, though all luster was gone, leaving it to resemble ash.

"Gone," Tania whispered, still at the door, refusing to enter. "Dead."

Hugh backed up from the bed, knowing he would take care of the mess later when she was safely away. It was his duty to protect her from such things. He shut the door, leading her away.

"William," she said, her voice still soft. Her body shuddered.

"Aye, I'll ask him whenever he deems to arrive."

"Nay, William is finally here. I feel him seeking entrance." Tania's wings beat harder as she flew toward the hall. Hugh walked fast to keep up with her, but short of full out running, he couldn't go her pace on foot. Once he turned his focus from the empty chamber of the dead faeries, he felt the faint trace of his brother's familiar energy in the distance.

Knowing Tania would show him the way, Hugh glanced around to make sure he was alone before letting his wings flap. He lifted off the floor, speeding down the stairwell with his fingertips gliding along the wall to keep his flight path straight, before landing just out of sight of the main hall.

"My sister!" William was saying as Hugh entered. The hall was empty as most of the faeries were outside the palace walls mending flowers, talking to the birds and sleeping with the blessed soldiers. William bowed low in Tania's direction as she fluttered over his head. "You grow more beautiful each time we meet."

Hugh hid his smile as Tania blushed and giggled at the compliment. "William, what took you so long?"

William wrinkled his nose. Wryly, and just to annoy his eldest sibling, he said, "Nice wings, brother."

"Aye, hello to you as well," Hugh drawled. "Now, tell us, where have you been? You're late. I've already been to King Merrick's. The spell and the potion did not work."

William's face fell and he looked to the side. "The delay was unavoidable, but naught for you to think on. I simply
60

misjudged... But, there is no reason to discuss it. I'm here now."

"How is Thomas? Bellemare? The horses? Has something happened?" Hugh watched his brother's every movement for a sign.

"Nay, they are all well," William said. "Prince Ladon is still in your place and none suspect the difference. How could they? They understand nothing of magic. Though, he is not you and never could be, his presence lends a calm to Bellemare. The horses we brought back from King Ean's encampment have bred well with the Bellemare stallions. The line is strengthening. Crops didn't do so well, or so our brother says, but none starve and all are content enough. I worry most for Thomas. He is not his cheery self, but that is to be expected, I suppose, with one brother estranged and a sister in stone."

"Did the scrolls give a clue as to how to free Juliana?" Hugh asked, a part of him aching to once more be able to see his beloved Bellemare. It stung that someone could be in his place, but Prince Ladon was a good man—being as he was blessed. Thomas could well handle all else. Still, Hugh missed his home.

"Naught that I haven't mentioned before. They confirm that if our sister truly did this to herself, the only way to free her will be what she wanted to be done." William motioned his hands to his sides, the long sleeves of his brown wizard robes swaying back and forth as he turned, stretching his back. "I've meditated on the matter and I don't think a purely magical solution is the key to freeing her. We need to know why she did it and then we might know the how."

Hugh's chest tightened. Tania looked at him in concern, sensing his pain. She started to move toward him, but he gave her a weak smile and signaled that he was all right. "How do we know what she was thinking? I don't understand anything Juliana's done since Merrick kidnapped her."

"Maybe it is not what she was thinking so much as what she wants." William sighed.

Hugh didn't like the look he gave him. "What do you think she wants?"

"What has always been the most important thing to our sister?" William glanced at Tania. She stared, wide-eyed, listening. "Family and the children of Bellemare. She went to Merrick because she believed the children were going to be harmed. Now that she carries her own inside her—"

"She'll want her family at peace before the child is born," Tania interrupted. "She'll want the whole land at peace."

"Nay," William said. "Juliana is used to war in the mortal realm. She has seen her brothers ride off into battle often. I doubt that she did this for the whole land. Methinks she did it for her family."

"She wants me to forgive Merrick." Hugh's guilt shimmered through him, dulling his faery magic and making his wings droop. Tania was instantly at his side, rubbing his arms with her small hands, trying to comfort him with her power. "My hatred caused this to happen."

William said nothing. He didn't have to.

"Are you hungry, William?" Tania asked, suddenly becoming a flurry of movement. Her wings fluttered and she called out to some of her faery ladies. "Lily, come, show William to a chamber. He is travel weary and should be—"

"Oh, aye," William broke in, excited. He knew well what it meant to be taken care of by a faery. "Very weary. Extremely weary."

A petite blonde fluttered forward, her white wings sparkling like stars against her dark blue dress. She was fair with soft white skin and a rose-tinted complexion. "Mm, I know what ails you, wizard. Come, bring your wand and let me work my magic on you."

Hugh watched them leave. A hand slipped over his arm and he looked down at his wife. Her eyes sparkled and little white lights floated around them, like snowflakes falling from her wings.

"We will not see William in the hall tonight," Tania said. "And all the faeries are gone to the forest to play."

Hugh understood her meaning and couldn't help the slight smile that crossed his lips as he pulled her into his embrace. He liked holding her. When she was in his arms, he knew she was safe. The euphoria of her embrace wrapped around his senses until all he could feel was her love. Every time she came near, he couldn't stop touching her. Hugh needed Tania like men needed air and blood.

When he went too long without her, his heart grew sad and his body weakened. She said it was the faery magic that linked them, but Hugh understood the feeling was buried much deeper. He would have been weak regardless of the magic. His heart beat only for her and his soul existed to be with hers.

"Let me help you forget your troubles, if only for a short time. There is naught to be done right now." Tania's long lashes fell heavy over her eyes. The come-hither look always got him, causing instant arousal to hasten his heartbeat and infuse his blood.

His shaft hard, Hugh reached for her, not caring that they were in the great hall of the Silver Palace. The sparkling walls seemed to dance with light as Tania lifted off the floor to join her mouth to his. Her lips parted in ready acceptance.

Reaching for her, Hugh felt her naked waist and drew back in mild surprise. Her clothing had changed from the gown to a sleek, midriff baring affair. It pulled tight to her breasts, hardly covering them. As always, her hair flowed about her shoulders the perfect frame to her lovely face. The skirt split slowly up the middle, revealing her long legs. Her bare feet didn't touch the ground. Once, when Hugh asked her why she never wore shoes, she said she liked feeling nature on her feet.

He groaned in arousal as his gaze traveled up her legs, following the splitting skirt to her exposed thighs and then higher to the teasing peek of her naked sex. His faery queen knew how to tease him, how to seduce his eyes and stir his body. At first, her revealing gowns bothered him when she wore them in front of others, but he'd since learned that faeries were not so modest as human women and it was a trait he could well appreciate.

The waist of the skirt revealed her navel, the small divot in her flesh making him lick his lips. He took a step forward, but she fluttered back, moving toward their thrones. The thin bodice clung to her budded nipples, the material becoming all the sheerer as he stared.

"It has been awhile since we had this hall to ourselves," Tania said.

Hugh pulled at his tunic, nearly ripping it in his haste to rid himself of clothes. His wing bent and he stretched it, unconsciously lifting his feet off the floor as he walked through the air to reach his wife. He tossed the tunic aside. Tania reached the throne, her playful smile full of promise as she sat.

"Kneel before me, my king." She parted her thighs. The skirt clung to her hips, but the slit allowed him to see the wet folds of her sex as they sparkled like her wings.

Hugh obeyed, coming to his knees before her. He grabbed her thighs and jerked her roughly forward. His lips parted, eager to taste her yet again. Each time he wanted her, he found her body wet and ready for him, her desires enough to match his own. With a groan, he licked along her slit, twirling his tongue over the sweet bud he found within. She moaned, responding like she always did.

Sweet, pretty sounds escaped her as his intimate kiss deepened. Unable to resist, he reached between his own thighs, dipping his hand beneath the waistband of his breeches to grab his erection. His fist pumped to the rhythm of his tongue.

"I want more," she commanded him.

Hugh broke away, the taste of her on his mouth as he pushed up from the floor. His lips captured hers, kissing her once more. Her tongue slid along the side of his, eliciting a moan. Running his hands along her waist, he jerked her top down to find her nipples were indeed hard. The material melted beneath his fingers only to disappear. Massaging her breast, he pinched the budded nipple.

Passionately, he drew his lips along her chin, nibbling lightly at her ear. Her breasts called to him and he couldn't resist capturing one in his mouth, greedily sucking and biting the hard nipple. Their magic erupted, like falling stars showering around them, impassioning them even more.

Tania's hands found his breeches, freeing him to her. He pressed her into the throne and she pushed at his arms. Her tone a breathless plea, she whispered, "Fly me into the air, my king."

His heart beat fast, choking all words from his throat as he lifted her into the air. Her wings helped to carry them upwards, high off the stone palace floor. As if sensing her will, their bodies poofed with a shower of magic, their figures becoming small and light as they were but specks against the giant great hall ceiling.

Hugh caressed her legs, ripping the slit of her skirt so that it fell away. Her small hand wrapped around his arousal, stroking it so delicately that it made him ache for the tight sheathe of her sex. Impatient with the need to claim her, he gripped her ass, pressing her along the high wall near the curved arch of the silver ceiling.

He stroked a finger along her sex, testing the silken depths of her need for him. Her skin was soft velvet to his harder flesh and unable to resist, he thrust his finger in and out.

"More," she commanded him.

Hugh obeyed, would always obey his queen. He gripped her hips firmly, angling himself as he pressed her into the wall. His feet dangled in the air, but his wings propelled him forward as he thrust. The great need he felt for her sped through his veins, drowning out all other thoughts and concerns.

Thrusting inside her warmth, he pumped his wings, holding her hips only to let go and let the pull of the ground force her body deep onto his. Never as a mortal did he imagine such feats as he'd done with his wife. Lights erupted around them, falling on the floor below.

Hugh withdrew, only to thrust once more. He controlled the pace, moving in and out, in and out, soaking in her soft sighs and whimpering moans. The tension built until he was desperate for release. Her breath caught and he felt her sex tighten around him, bringing her sweet climax. The pull of her muscles beckoned him to join and he did, spilling his seed deep inside her fragile body.

Tania's cry joined his and he held her tight, keeping her pressed against the smooth palace ceiling. Here, in this moment, no other thing mattered. They were together, hidden from the world, hidden from the concerns of their rule, of their family. She was his haven and he clung to her, never wanting to let go.

Chapter Four

King Lucien didn't move, hadn't moved for some time. Fires burned bright and hot in his bedchamber—in the oversized fireplace, in basins, on candles and torches—but he did not feel the heat. Inside he was cold.

Light gauze hung from the ceiling, fluttering noiselessly around the room. The material was scorched from old flames, hanging like thick, old spider webs coated in ash. Though the material occasionally blew close to the flames, it did not catch fire. It only burned when he willed it to. The sheer cloth fluttered before his face, hiding Mia's prone body from his gaze. He waited, not leaning to the side to see her.

Once, his bedchamber, indeed his whole Fire Palace, had held a dark beauty in its décor. He made it that way for her, for his nymph. He gave her every comfort, keeping her safe in his bedchamber. Whatever she needed, she was given and all he asked in return was her utter obedience. But then she betrayed him, and not just once, but several times. She freed two of his prized prisoners from the dungeons—Prince Ladon and William the Wizard. When he had Hugh and Tania in his grasp, she helped them escape. She warned Bellemare that his demons were coming. She even freed Sir Nicholas, not that it did much good. The man came crawling back, begging to have his soul extracted. Lucien took it, and gladly, because of Nicholas' intimate knowledge of the Bellemare family.

The scorched material moved again, unveiling Mia's unmoving form amongst the dark furs of his bed. The worst betrayal was when she kissed William the Wizard. Though much time had passed, he still felt the pain of it in the pit of his stomach. She betrayed him and it only made him want her more.

As she escaped, he'd been sure she'd leave with the man. He waited for her to go. To his surprise, she stayed. But by her own words, he knew she stayed out of fear and because he had her soul. She did not stay because that is what she wanted.

Lucien hadn't wanted to be reminded of beauty's treacherous face, her easy lies, so he let Anja take his nymph to the dungeons. When Mia was below, he had time to focus his energies into his kingdom. With each passing day, his obsession with her absence empowered him even as it tortured. He was the Damned King. He could have any women he wanted, by either seduction or force. And yet he held back, letting his own torment feed the evil power inside him.

In his darkest hours, those he'd normally spend with his imprisoned lover, he'd almost ordered Anja to kill Mia and thus purge himself of her forever. He could not. The soothsayer predicted he was to have a son, a child that would lead his army of half-breeds into the mortal realm and conquer it. Mia would be the child's mother.

"You didn't leave with him." Lucien's voice was soft. "You didn't leave with William. You could have tried, but you chose to stay with me."

Mia didn't answer, unable to hear him as he willed her to stay asleep. She looked thin from her ordeal down in the dungeons, but he knew Anja had not tortured her—at least physically. He'd ordered it so, using the excuse that if she was to carry his dark prince then she'd need to be unharmed.

"You could have tried to escape. Instead you came here to my bed. Does this mean you accept your fate?"

Still no answer, but Lucien didn't need one. She didn't accept him, only the knowledge of his power over her. He had half her soul and she would be a fool to try and escape him. No matter where she went, he would find her. He would always find her.

"She is the reason why you have failed in the past. That nymph makes you weak. Let me take her back to the dungeons where she cannot distract you."

Lucien had felt the evil behind him and when Anja spoke, he turned to look at her. "The faeries?"

She pouted a lip at his refusal to talk about Mia. "They are here. I had them delivered to the great hall. You should hear their moans, so much anguish." Anja giggled, delighted by her own words. "The evil that Sir Nicholas left planted inside them has made their souls raw with pain."

"Who would have thought the mortal would have done something right in innocently taking faeries to his bed?" Lucien chuckled. When he'd sent the demon to possess Nicholas, answering the man's plea and helping him to kill his father, he never expected him to be more than a diversion. Lucien only knew of Nicholas because of his connection to the Bellemare family. And now, instead of trying to tempt them from afar, that single murder drew the Bellemare into the Immortal Realm. Juliana to Merrick, torturing the Unblessed King now from the stone prison Merrick tried to keep secret. Hugh to Feia, bitten by the living dead and unable to return to Bellemare. Now that the Bellemare family was connected to his world, they would not find their way out so easily.

"His touch has poisoned them," Anja said. "All three will carry a seed of your demon army. Their wombs are ripe. We must act tonight and extract their souls before the evil kills them. We cannot let their souls escape in death. I have summonsed your most powerful warriors, those of the purest breeds, and have told them to ready their human temples. The children cannot be born in this world. The other kingdoms cannot know what we do. We will hide the children and their mothers in the mortal realm."

"The others are busy with their war," Lucien said. "They won't sense the evil army until it is well upon them."

"A war you instigated." Anja clapped. "And now they're all so sad and distracted. No one pays attention to us."

"You are too kind, soothsayer." Lucien arched a brow, strolling toward the child. "But you brought me Juliana's knife. You helped to trap her in a realm of stone."

"Aye, I did. And there she will wait until we are ready to steal the child from her." The child giggled. "Soon my spirits will chase her to our dungeon and I will trap her there. But for now, they tease her, whispering naughty little things into her lonely ears."

"The Unblessed King will not recover so easily from the loss." Lucien grinned. "You are too cunning, evil seer."

The child smiled, swaying back and forth on her feet, only to stop. Her face fell and she gave him a wry look. "You want something from me. Your compliments are too pretty."

Lucien laughed. It took her long enough to catch on to his ploy.

"What?" She put her hand on her hips and tapped her toes in waiting. "What is it you want?"

"I want you to bring the crone to my hall. I want to meet her."

71

"She only speaks to me." Anja shook her head in denial.

"I want to meet her."

"Why?"

"I wish to ask her something."

"Ask me." Anja pouted.

"But you're only a child. I want the crone."

Anja's face wrinkled in anger, her skin reddening as her true nature began to show itself. Her silken hair began to harden, becoming brittle. "Are you saying I have not enough power?"

Lucien saw her impudence and released the tight hold he kept on the demon inside. His eyes filled with the darkness and he felt the crimson streaks burning their way through the black. Like the scorched embers of a dying fire, his flesh crackled to an ashen gray.

"I will speak to her," Anja rushed, not giving him time to build his rage more. "I cannot promise she will come, but I will try to persuade her."

"Wise decision. Now, let us go barter for the faery souls." Lucien gave the seer a small smile. Though he wanted to, he did not look at Mia again as he left his chambers. Anja skipped behind him, humming a little tune only she knew the words to. "I wouldn't want to keep the demon sires waiting."

༄༅༎

Juliana took a deep breath, shivering as she huddled against the protruding edge of the large, barren fireplace in the great hall of the Black Palace. The dark spirits were stirring, their shadowed bodies drifting over the land of stone as if searching for her. So long as she didn't move, they wouldn't find her.

"He forgets you." The whisper tickled the back of her ear, causing her to bite her lip hard as the spirit glided past. It didn't stop, not detecting her exact spot. She heard the whisper repeating as the shadows slipped away. A tear slid over her cheek.

"He doesn't forget," she mouthed, no sound coming as she thought the words in her head. "Hear me, Merrick. See me again. Bring me back to you. Bring me back."

Merrick opened his eyes, sleep not coming as he felt Juliana all around him. The sweet smell of her body invaded his nose, tempting him with desire. When he cast the spell to bring her to his bed, he thought to do so to find comfort in her memory. Instead, the spell tormented him because it wasn't real. It was a manifestation of his memory of her, an elusive peek at what he wanted most.

Still, as his thoughts turned, tempted by her familiar scent, the echoing of her soft voice in the back of his mind, he didn't resist. Lying still so that the sensations could take hold, he waited for when the feel of her hands would join the other sensations.

His blood stirred with arousal. He didn't fight the passion as his shaft grew heavy between his thighs, pressing against the coverlet on his bed. The moment he detected her scent, he'd willed the clothes to disappear from his body, leaving him naked. His limbs were sprawled on the large bed, waiting, eager.

Sensing Juliana's fear, he called to it, urging her to come to him. He wanted her, always wanted her, and the knowledge that he couldn't simply will her to appear before him irritated to no end. She was his and Merrick wanted her back. From the beginning, from the first time he saw her in the Mortal Realm, he'd been obsessed with her. He thought by bringing her to his palace, making her his queen, the obsession would leave him. It only became worse until he'd rather cut out his own heart than go on without her.

Obsession led to madness and the creatures of Valdis wouldn't follow a mad king obsessed with a woman, a former human no less. The war with Tegwen raged on, demanding he be strong. There were many who would gladly relieve him of his throne, leaving Juliana trapped and the seat of unblessed power open. Only death would relinquish him of his crown and no matter how he tired of life, he didn't wish for death. He must live for Juliana, for the hope that one day he'd have her before him once more. Whether, upon that reunion, he rung her neck or kissed her endlessly would remain to be seen.

"You promised to stay with me," he whispered, as the gliding touch of her hand found his stomach. At first it was light, like the subtle caress of a warm breeze, but as the stroke pushed upward, it became harder. Nails caught on his flesh, giving a bit of pain to his pleasure. He welcomed it, knowing in those hands was the same urgency his body felt.

Stay with me, Juliana. Stay.

"Stay," Juliana urged Merrick, knowing instinctively that he couldn't hear her, just as she couldn't hear him. But it had to be his body that called to her. His hands hesitated before reaching up to touch her sides. The swell of her stomach hadn't stopped his desire for her in the least. Whenever this happened, whenever his spirit called, she was pulled to their bedchamber to be with his ghostly image. Though transparent to look at, he was solid to touch and she did, eagerly running her hands over his thick muscles, soaking in what comfort she could. Once they found release, his image would fade and she'd be alone on the bed, dressed and aching for more time.

But she wouldn't think about that now. Naked, Juliana straddled his thighs with her knees, looking down onto his transparent face. The soft fur of a coverlet separated them and she pressed her knees tight against him. These brief moments in his bed were all she had and she clung to them desperately.

"Merrick," she whispered, wishing he could hear her. All he did was touch and she wondered if that was all he could do, or if he was indeed punishing her for trying to end the immortal war. Still, for all her doubt, she couldn't refuse him.

Nothing else mattered in these sweet, short moments. The fear she felt of the spirits down in the hall disappeared. With him, even a ghostly him, she felt safe. Juliana ran her hands over his chest to his neck, moving up to stroke his achingly handsome face. Each delicately sunken curve, each perfect bend of flesh pulled at her heart. So much time had passed and yet, when she touched him, she could forget years. There was only Merrick and Juliana, two lovers, bound eternally.

She willed him to solidify, to become whole so she might hear the sound of his voice, see the exact shade of his tanned skin. Her wish wasn't granted and she was left with the rapid pants of her breath as she leaned into him, only to hear the hollow beat of her heart in her ears.

His erection probed her from beneath the coverlet, making her stomach knot in a mixture of anticipation and dread, for each second drew her closer to the end when his warm hands would leave her and she'd be left on her bed of stone. A mist grew around them, rolling like fog from the ocean, to blur the chamber walls. It grew above the bed, cocooning them in a private alcove. He squeezed her hips, his dark eyes piercing into her, never closing in rapture as he watched her face.

Unable to resist, Juliana kissed him, her eyes open to look deep into his, as if she could read his thoughts. She searched for his soul, only to see her own mirrored back at her. The taste of him invaded her mouth. It was the subtle, warm spice of the ale he enjoyed before bed. The intimate caress intoxicated her senses more than ale ever could.

Moaning, she cupped his face, controlling the movement of the kiss. She dipped her tongue along the edge of his mouth, teasing him until he became aggressive. His hands roamed over the back of her thighs, around her ass to skim the length of her spine. Fingers wrapped the back of her neck, holding her down against him.

Juliana leaned her weight on one hand and knee, tugging at the fur to pull it down on one side and then the other. With full access to his body, she tore her mouth away with a gasp. Still, there was no sound coming from him, though his transparent lips moved and the memory of his voice stirred in the back of her mind.

"Juliana," he would whisper and she'd know he loved her, though he never said the words. It was in the way he said her name. "Juliana."

She touched everywhere she could reach, placing open-mouthed kisses against his throat, enjoying the taste of his flesh. Her hands skimmed over his budded nipples and as if sensing her aching need, he mimicked her movements, rubbing her breasts in his strong hands. With each pinch of the sensitive peaks, a twinge of desire erupted in her sex.

"Merrick," she moaned, knowing no one would hear her and yet strangely comforted by the sound of her hoarse voice. "Merrick, please stay with me. Don't go."

As if by silent understanding, they took it slow, stretching out the movements. Legs brushed against legs, intertwining. The stiff length of his arousal pressed up into her, as if begging for attention. She reached between his thighs, her hand gliding onto his shaft.

The instant she touched the smooth, tight flesh, Merrick flipped her onto her back, trapping her fingers against him. He rocked his hips into her hand, massaging himself against her eager fingers.

His mouth opened and she felt his breath flutter along her skin, an intimate whisper that caused her desperate heart to ache. Juliana dug her fingertips into his chest, willing him to feel her agony, to free her from her stony prison. Why did he wait? Why?

His body jerked, signifying he felt the clawing of her nails. Juliana did it again, harder than before. Merrick became impassioned, his body restlessly moving along hers as he gripped her thighs, forcing them open. His lips wrapped around a puckered nipple, biting gently. Juliana's head rolled back into the cushioned bed. Her hips searched for the contact of his.

And then he lifted, angling himself so that he could better enter her. The tip of his arousal brushed along her folds, parting them. She tensed, ready for that first push of him entering her, filling her, completing her. When he moved, it was perfection.

"Merrick, please, bring me back to you. I want to be with you. I love you." Juliana forced her eyes to stay open, not wanting to miss a single instant of his determined face as he took her slow and steady. Each thrust stirred her desire even as it tormented. She squirmed, arching to meet him. And, as the first tremors of her climax rained over her, she fought her release. To find the bliss of orgasm only brought the aftermath of despair.

"Merrick, please, keep me with you. I don't want to go."

Juliana gasped. She could not fight their climax any more than she could fight loving him. When it came, the bittersweet torment flowed over her in perfect waves. Right as she peaked, heart beating wildly, she grabbed for his arms, trying to hold on. Her hands fell into air, unable to keep her intangible husband no matter how hard she tried.

"Nay," she cried, as the bed beneath her hardened. The fog pulled away, leaving her alone in her stone prison. Tears streamed over her cheeks in wet, hot trails. "Please, nay. Merrick, do not leave me."

Merrick groaned as his body fell through the transparent image of his wife, sinking into the soft mattress still warm from her body. His pillow smelled of her and he buried his face into it, breathing her in, trying to keep her with him. But, like always, the scent of her dissipated, leaving him completely alone with only the memory to torment him.

Feeling a sting on his chest, he pushed up. Juliana had been almost violent this time as they came together, clawing into him like never before. Pushing up, he reached for his chest, wondering why he could still feel the sting even after she was gone. When he pulled his hand back, there was blood on it.

Merrick darted to his feet, materializing a mirror alongside his bed. Angry scratches stared back at him, spelling backward letters in his flesh.

"Get me out," he read, stunned.

It wasn't a dream. Juliana had been real, she was with him and if the bleeding words on his chest were any indication, she wanted him to get her back. Now.

Chapter Five

Bellemare Castle, England, Mortal Realm

Thomas watched his brother, the Earl of Bellemare, woo yet another chambermaid away from her duties. The woman was pale and slender, but her cheeks were rosy with health and beauty. She was merely one of the pretty women who lived within the castle. It wasn't arranged like that on purpose, but merely an effect of Bellemare's magical blessing. All prospered, even the serfs and servants.

The tallest of all the siblings, Hugh's very presence emitted nobility and power in his dark green tunic with gold trim. The Bellemare crest—a black stallion statant on a field of green— was embroidered onto the chest, echoed in the dark green emerald of his ring. All of the Bellemare siblings had dark brown hair that gleamed in the sunlight, high cheekbones and proud features. The oldest, Hugh, and the youngest, William, both had brown eyes as dark as sin. Juliana and Thomas had blue eyes the color of the night sky, taking after their long passed mother.

Looking at the earl, Thomas saw his entire life reflected back at him. He saw them as children, playing in Bellemare's grassy pastures. They used to ride their horses through the fields until the animals could barely breathe, and then they themselves would run until every nook and crack in the land

and castle were as familiar as their own faces. They hid from each other, carved names in the dark stone entryway of the outer bailey wall. The brothers taught Juliana how to fight in the courtyard. Thomas kissed his first maid in the stables, made love to her days later behind the brewery.

But, no matter the memories seeing the earl's face invoked, it wasn't his brother, Hugh, standing before him. He looked like him, talked like him and with Thomas' help even acted like him. Yet, it wasn't him. He was an imposter; one Thomas helped to keep in Lord Hugh's place.

Blue tapestries hung on the wall, along with a banner of the Bellemare crest. A large stone fireplace set along the wall opposite the head table. A fire burned brightly, giving the hall light when the sun shining through the iron-grated windows would not, or when the oak shutters were closed. There were also many candles, made from animal fat and beeswax, placed along spikes in the stone walls.

Thomas was seated at his place next to Sir Geoffery at the head table where the family and honored guests dined, though the table felt somewhat empty as of late. They were lifted above the rest of the hall on a platform. Below the high table, the permanent dining tables and benches were set up for the servants, soldiers and freemen of the keep. Though currently empty, servants readied the tables for the evening meal. The fact that the tables were permanent fixtures in the manor, and not the usual portable kind, showed the extent of the Bellemare wealth.

"It gladdens my heart to see the earl no longer mopes about the castle." Sir Geoffrey was a steadfast knight, one the Bellemare brothers would trust with their lives. As children, they'd all trained for knighthood under the same lord. With his dark skin, hazel eyes and short cropped hair, he didn't look like a Bellemare, but he was one of them. He lived in the castle, led the Bellemare knights and guarded their lands when the brothers were away. The man even knew the secrets of Bellemare—of the other world hidden where most humans could not see, of the blessing bestowed upon it by an ancient elfin king because his daughter had been turned mortal, of the magical creatures that helped protect that blessing and of the half demons who would see it end.

"Aye," Thomas agreed, though he didn't sound enthusiastic. Geoffrey might be a close friend, but one thing he didn't know about was Hugh's double. Thomas had promised his brother not to tell unless it became necessary and, in his desire to not disappoint his brother, he'd kept that promise.

"Are you troubled because he takes the pretty maids from your bed?" Geoffrey chuckled as he lifted a goblet to his mouth. He took a long drink of mead.

Thomas kept his eye on the pretend Hugh, not speaking. After fifty years of torment in Lucien's prison, Ladon had wanted to escape the Immortal Realm. Thomas was afraid of losing Bellemare to demons. With Hugh gone, everything was his responsibility—the keep, the land, the famous Bellemare horses, the people.

"A strange thing occurs to me, Sir Thomas," Geoffrey continued thoughtfully. "You both came back from the Otherworld and it is as if your souls are switched. He loves the women and you brood as he once did. Though overly serious, he seems more carefree and I see you carrying the burden of the title."

Thomas snorted. What could he say? It was true. Only, unlike Hugh who had brooded because he loved the faery queen and thought he couldn't have her, Thomas now brooded about the things he could not change. He was alone. For the first time in his life he felt without family. Juliana was frozen in stone.

Hugh was trapped in the Immortal Realm unable to come back even for a visit without dying. William was distracted and of very little comfort, even when he was home. Not saying the whole truth, he answered, "My head does not let me sleep. I fight demons in my dreams."

"The nightmares haven't stopped?"

They've become worse, Thomas thought, before answering aloud, "They are only dreams and with time they will cease. I'm not the first man to have nightmares after a battle."

"You are the first I know to have nearly died in a battle against goblins and trolls in the Otherworld. What are the dreams about?"

"They're strange. I feel myself flying through a pair of old, decrepit doors in a gate, surrounded by demons who are trying to grab hold. I'm me, but the breeze flows through me and when a demon does touch, it burns the flesh. Never you mind, it makes no sense."

"Such is the way of dreams." Geoffrey thankfully respected Thomas' need to talk of other things. "However, something else troubles me more than nightmares."

Thomas arched a brow.

"I know you are Sir Thomas. You know the stories from our childhood. If I come at you with a sword, you know how to defend yourself against me. You know my weakness for redheads and I your preference for pretty women in general." Geoffrey again took a drink. Then, tipping the edge of his goblet across the main hall in Hugh's direction, he sighed. "I know all these things, as do you, but what I would know is, who it is I have been calling 'my lord'."

That brought Thomas out of his contemplative stupor. Blinking, he turned to his friend.

"Nay, do not protest it. I've thought long and hard over this matter and that man, though he does speak and look like Lord Hugh, he is no more the earl than I am that serving wench he is courting." Setting down the goblet, Geoffrey frowned slightly. Another maid joined the man as they watched, simpering prettily as she fought for his attention. "It's hard to say what first made me realize it. There were small things. He moves unlike Hugh, uses strange words and fights differently. Today, to test him, I attacked using one of the first, simple techniques we learned. He couldn't defend against it and I nearly took off his head."

Thomas didn't even try to deny the claim. "His name is Ladon. He is a blessed prince disguised as my brother so none from his world can find him and none from ours will know of Hugh's..."

"The earl is dead?" Geoffrey sat up straighter. His face paled, as he stared at Thomas. "How—?"

"Nay, only dead to this realm. When we fought that demon shaped as Lord Eadward and Hugh was bitten, he became infected. The creature is called a living dead and Hugh cannot return or he'll die from his wound." It actually felt good being able to tell someone the truth.

Geoffrey sat back, his mouth slightly agape in shock. "I suspected something like that for awhile now, but to hear you say it..."

"Had you not said anything, I would not have spoken of it," Thomas admitted. "I promised Hugh to help the prince adjust to the position, until such a time as he can return to his realm and we can effectively fake my brother's death and name me the successor."

"Hmm." Geoffrey rubbed his temple thoughtfully.

"Aye." Thomas nodded.

"Does my lord live with Lady Juliana?"

"Nay, he rules the Kingdom of Feia. There, with Queen Tania, he will live forever."

"The earl is a king?" Geoffrey smiled, nodding in approval. "It is very fitting. He will make a fine ruler."

Thomas smirked. "King of the faeries. He even has their magic."

Geoffrey chuckled. "Ah, now that is something I would give my sword arm to see. Hugh with wings."

"I didn't see any wings," Thomas admitted, "but his breeches did sparkle a little last I saw him."

Geoffrey laughed so hard he snorted.

"I'm sorry I didn't tell you about him, but—" Thomas began, only to stop when Geoffrey lifted his hand and shook his head, indicating there was no need to explain. Before he could again speak, Thomas felt a tug on his leg. His first instinct was to lightly kick, thinking a dog had gotten into the castle, but when he looked down he saw wide blue eyes gazing up at him. They were almost too big for the face. Rees, the Bellemare spright, was one of the magical creatures who worked at the keep. He wore a bright green tunic that fell to his thighs and his unkempt, short brown hair stood on end. "Aye?"

"I counted the hairs of the new steed and they are five short in the tail." Rees looked distressed. "Not four or three or six, but five."

"Aye?" Thomas repeated, glancing up at Geoffrey. The knight motioned his hand weakly, unconcerned. It wasn't the first time Rees came to them with some inane story about the horses.

"Giles was in the stables earlier," Rees said. "He is not to be in the stables."

"Aye?" Thomas knew the spright often fought with Giles, the household brownie who lived in the castle pantry, or more accurately, in a barrel of ale in the castle pantry.

"And a faery brought a message vial." Rees reached into his breeches and pulled out a vial filled with blue liquid. He shook it violently. "From King Hugh of the Faeries. I told her we had a Hugh here and she laughed, asking if I'd been swimming in the ale barrel because she smelled ale."

"Huh?" Thomas asked, partly because the spright was talking so fast and partly because he found some small amusement in teasing him.

"Giles was in the barn," Rees said slowly.

"Aye." Thomas tried to hide his grin.

"Giles smells of ale."

"Aye."

"Harrumph!" Rees again lifted the vial, shaking it at the table in the direction of the pretend earl. "And I told you that was not Lord Hugh. I know the earl and that is an imposter. Hugh is now a king. A king! And he did not call me to be by his side. Me! His spright!"

"What is happening today?" Thomas muttered, only to say to the spright, "That imposter is Prince Ladon of Tegwen."

"Ah, so that's the surge of magic I've been feeling around the castle. You two have been casting protection spells over the keep, haven't you? Methought they were a sight too powerful for just William."

"Aye, we have," Thomas said. "To assure we keep the demons out. Hugh knew you would understand that he needed you here to help the blessed prince, being as you are a blessed creature and you are his spright. That is why you are still here."

"Ah." Rees chewed his lip thoughtfully. Gradually, he nodded, a smile crossing his features. Sighing in what could only be relief, he added, "And I bet he sent a faery to tell me this, only the daft creatures forgot or lost their way." He lowered his voice to a whisper. "Constantly flitting about the soldiers, they are. They lost my missive from the king. I have half a mind to tell King Hugh what they did. I'm sure he will not be happy to hear his spright was not told of this matter."

"May I see the message?" Thomas held out his hand toward the spright. Normally the vials were delivered directly to William, but the youngest brother was in the Immortal Realm with Hugh.

"Oh, aye." Rees tossed the missive vial at Thomas, only to hop onto the table. Imposter Hugh glanced in the spright's direction, but the maids he currently charmed didn't indicate they saw the tiny magical creature. Rees hopped down, ran across the floor and leapt onto the prince's shoulder, tugging at his ear. His mouth opened and closed at a fast rate, as if he chattered incessantly in Ladon's ear. The prince tried to continue smiling, but it was obvious by the way he swatted at the spright that he was distracted from his purpose.

"Did Lord Hugh send Rees a message and order him to help the prince?" Geoffrey asked when they were alone, pushing his goblet away.

"Nay." Thomas shook his head in denial and stood. He motioned Geoffery to follow, as he led the way from the hall to the circular stairwell that led out to the bailey yard below. "But the creature would not let up if we did not tell him as much. The truth is, Hugh is probably glad to be rid of the spright. Blind admiration makes him uncomfortable."

Thomas glanced up as they walked into the yard lit by evening sun. The limed white stone of the castle took on an orange cast. In front of the castle was the courtyard. The castle itself set atop a motte of earth and rock. It towered a good fifty feet above the bailey. A taller wall, constructed of stone and timber, ringed around the inner bailey to guard the main part of the keep.

"Is that the magical message you were telling me about?" Sir Geoffrey motioned at the blue-filled vial in Thomas' hand.

"Aye," Thomas answered, continuing past the bailey wall. He glanced under the gateway toward the outer yard. Beyond the wall a second, lower wall made the outer perimeter. The only way in and out of the yard was through the front gatehouse and currently the guards were at their posts, standing upright and alert.

Contained within the inner courtyard was the exercise yard for the knights, a small chapel, the newly built stables, a barn, a few workshops, and a small brewery. Thomas walked alongside the inner courtyard, toward the stables. After the old building burned down during a demon attack where horses were killed, everyone in the castle made a concerted effort to keep a sharp eye on the new one—not that they knew an actual demon caused the fire. To many it was an accident, the last in a line of very unfortunate events which, though attributed to the devil, could not be proved beyond faith.

"Are you going to see what Hugh has to say?" Geoffrey again eyed the vial.

"I want to check on the horses." Thomas heard the animals in their stalls for the evening. "The missives always say the same thing, urging William to hurry and find a cure for our sister or telling us whatever he's tried hasn't worked."

The stable boy bowed, immediately moving toward the back to give the two men privacy. Going to his horse's stall, Thomas patted the animal's muzzle. Known as the Bellemares, the breed was an ancient mix of bloodlines, a cross-breeding of French trotters and hunters for stamina, with the intelligence of a Holstein Warmblood and the jumping abilities of a Lipizzaner. There was also some Arabian blood in the English stock. And, the newest addition, a magical elfin breed brought from the Immortal Realm to help replenish the stock after the fire. To the common ear, it sounded like a hodgepodge, but the men of Bellemare knew horses.

Like the others, Thomas' stallion had a distinctly simple chestnut coloring to its coat with a dark stripe down the back from shoulder blades to tail. The horse's hair and eyes were also dark chestnut, making it nearly invisible at night.

"Cure?" Geoffrey reached for the animal, petting the side of its neck. "What is this about Lady Juliana?"

"There is more I should explain." Thomas stared into the horse's eyes, not wanting to look at his friend as he felt the responsibility of his family on his head. Hugh's responsibility was now his. He was Bellemare.

"Aye, methinks you should, Thomas," Geoffrey agreed. "I have a feeling there is much you need to tell me."

CRECRED

"So you are the crone who gives my little Anja such wonderful presents." Lucien lifted his hand to materialize the jeweled dagger that had belonged to Queen Juliana. He let the demon have control, knowing the creature to be fiercely persuasive if not deeply impressive. Besides, with the beast in control, he didn't have to feel Mia upstairs, in his bed, waiting. "A fine dagger it is, too."

The Damned King smiled at the frail, blind witch kneeling before him in the main hall of the Fire Palace, bidding her with a subtle tipping of the knife blade to stand. Her eyes were missing from her head and a band of dirty white material covered the sockets, pulling tight to her short white hair. Despite this, she didn't need eyes to see him. Her dingy linen gown was tattered from many years of wear. He could feel her strong power, running deeper than Anja's. And, as the soothsayer neared the old woman to embrace her, he felt their combined powers growing. Not really old woman and child, the two were born from the same dark magic that fed his reign. They were manifestations of the darkest desires and most hateful lusts.

When the witch spoke, her low words were enunciated and raw, "And you are the new Damned King. A pleasure that our magics should finally meet. Let me offer you some of King Merrick's pain as tribute."

The witch held out her hand, letting a thin strip of power twirl off her fingertips. As it touched him, Lucien instantly smelled Merrick. He tasted the agony and frustration the Unblessed King felt in seeing Juliana's stone prison. It was a potent taste of evil magic and he was empowered by it, knowing Merrick suffered still. Queen Juliana had kept Merrick from joining the damned completely, being as the Unblessed King was always teetering between blessed and damned. Now, with Juliana gone, it was only a matter of time before Merrick came to the Damned King to beg for her back. He felt King Merrick was close to crumbling and laughed to know it.

"A great tribute you bring me, witch, and a great many plans you have laid while imprisoned by the Unblessed King," Lucien said.

"Once Merrick's bride succumbed to the fears I cast over her, she rearranged my prison just enough to let me out. It is how I can now come to visit my sweet Anja in your very lovely dungeon. So many delightful screams, so much agony, so much torture." The crone nodded in approval. "And my Anja knows how to bring them forth with such precision."

"And what would you have of me in return?" Without waiting for her to answer, he lifted his hand. A new gown appeared on the woman's body, as fine as any faery princess. The cloth around her eyes shifted to match. She reached down, feeling the shimmering material, her bony fingers sliding along her waist. She grinned, nodding in approval. "A witch as fine and powerful as you should not be kept in such rags."

"I want one too!" Anja demanded, stamping her foot. The crone chuckled, reaching out to pat her head, not needing to see her to know where the child was.

"Very well, seer," Lucien allowed.

Nodding once, he gave Anja a gown to match the old woman's. She clapped her hands, jumping up and down, before holding her arms to the side, pretending like she was flying around the room. A loud moan sounded, followed by panted breaths, to interrupt their conversation.

"This is tiresome," Lucien growled, his voice echoing his frustration off the hall's ceiling. Flames wrapped around his ashen flesh, sinking into the black pits of his eyes. A mouthful of fangs rubbed along the inside of his mouth and he bit down, causing his lips to bleed. He drew the flames down his arm to his hand, bouncing a ball in his palm as he turned to eye the three faeries on the floor before them.

Their limbs were free, laying limp on the hard stone. There was no need for chains, for there was no escaping the Fire Palace now that he had them—not that they would have been able to find the strength to get away.

"Are these the first?" the witch asked with interest.

"Aye," Anja answered. "All three suffer from a dark affliction, one that will end in only two choices. Either they trade their souls to our king for immortality or they give in to the pain and die a horrific death."

"Both would be a pleasure to watch." The crone nodded in approval. "Only one serves a darker purpose."

Anja skipped to the three faeries. Pointing at the first, she said, "This one with the pale yellow wings that do not flutter is named Jolynne." She moved to the next. "And she with the blue, which have grayed with little use, is Leliah." The child moved to sit on the stomach of the last, patting her on the face. "And this is Nyda, with her green wings rotting like the decayed leaves on the forest ground. Pretty in her rot, is she not? Rot, not, rot, rot."

"Aye, lovely," the crone agreed, sounding very much like a tolerant and proud grandmother to a young child.

"Open your eyes and look," Anja whispered to the green faery, her voice so innocent the faeries on the floor could not help but obey her. All three shallow gazes moved slowly around, taking in the thin columns leading up to the ceiling, to the rough, black stalactites with their jagged sharp edges. The ceiling was tall, but like the rest of his palace, they were subject to Lucien's whims. With one inclination, the Damned King could call those spikes down to pierce the faeries' hearts. Anja stood once more, swinging her hips to make the skirt of her gown dance in the firelight. "If you do not ask, he cannot give. Do you want to die, sweet, sad faeries? Ask him and he can take the pain. No more hurt. No more sadness. Only pleasure eternal."

"Your innocence is truly deceitful, soothsayer." The Demon King laughed, the raspy sound again echoing, causing the blue faery to whimper.

By Lucien's will, a large bonfire surged in the circular pit in the middle of the hall. The edges of the floor lifted up slightly around the flames, as if the stone had been rolled over to make the fiery centerpiece. Eerie orange light cast over the prone, delicate beings. He felt their resistance to them when they first awoke to face him, just as he now felt that resistance faltering as their pain grew.

"The body might die," Leliah whispered, her voice hoarse and cracking with each word, "but the soul cannot be bartered."

"I knew you would be the difficult one," Lucien growled menacingly, standing over the blue-winged beauty. Even in her frail state, he felt the fire of good in her soul.

"You are a demon," she answered. "Naught you say to me I will hear."

Lucien laughed. He knelt on the floor, touching Leliah's pale face. He traced a sharpened nail along her cheek, taking some of her pain into himself. "Not always a demon, sweet one. Once I had a soul, a horrible, painful, pleasure-sucking soul. I promise you, it is nothing to miss."

"I will," came a whisper.

Lucien turned his sharp attention to the yellow-winged Jolynne. "What was that, sweet faery?"

"I will trade." Jolynne's voice shook.

"Will you?" Lucien chuckled, edging along the floor toward her, his knees bent and his fingertips holding part of his weight as he half-crawled, half-walked.

"I beg you, my king, take my soul to end the pain." Jolynne closed her eyes, gasping and panting as a tear streamed over her cheek. "I do not wish for death for I know not what is on the other side."

"Nay, Jolynne! He lies," Leliah screamed, finding more of her voice. "Only a devil's eyes burn in such a way. He lies. Lies!"

"This one is lost." Anja rested her hand on the screaming one's head. The faery tried to pull away, but the soothsayer's touch wasn't thrown off. "She will not succumb. I see it clearly."

"Aye, she will not," the crone agreed, not moving. "My Anja is right, that one is lost."

Lucien sighed in frustration. "Very well."

Falling stones sprinkled along the floor like rain, dropping around the blue faery. Leliah closed her eyes tight. The earth shook, the ceiling cracking in a jagged pattern across its great length. Suddenly, a stalactite broke free, falling from above. The sharpened tip pierced through the faery's stomach, stabbing through the floor with its huge size. She didn't scream, merely clenched her teeth for the brief, painful instant before death.

"You showed mercy," Anja accused, sounding almost embarrassed by his actions as she looked at the crone.

"If she will not ask, then I will no longer listen to her sniffling cries," Lucien growled.

"A Demon King should feed off the cries off the dying, not vanquish them," the soothsayer said.

"I am the king and I will feed off what I wish and that one had little left. Now bother me no more about such petty things or I will feed off you." Lucien glared at the child, knowing she tried to impress their old guest but not caring to be the victim of her insolence.

"There is no soul in me to feed off of," Anja grumbled in her little girl pout.

"Nevertheless," Lucien warned.

"I will trade," Jolynne repeated, over and over again. "I will trade. End the pain. End. Please, end."

Anja moved to the dead faery. Reaching for the tips of the blue wings, she pulled, ripping them off by the root. Setting them on the floor, she laid down on them, adhering them to her back with the faery's blood. When she stood, they drooped from her back, fluttering in the breeze as she ran in circles like a little girl at play.

"Ask me to end the pain in trade for your soul," Lucien instructed Jolynne, turning his attention from the seer.

"Aye, end it," the faery begged. "Take my soul."

"I accept, little one." Lucien stroked back her golden hair. "Do not be scared, I have great purpose for you."

Time stopped, all of them kept within a single instant. Flames did not move or crackle as the hall was left with the silence of the grave. Color faded, drained from the passing moment. Jolynne didn't move, but her eyes stayed on Lucien's face, pleading for the pain to stop. Next to her Nyda watched.

Anja clapped, jumping up and down, her new wings flopping to the floor behind her. She pouted her bottom lip, picking the fallen wings up and running to the crone so that the old woman could pat them back onto her blood streaked back.

The Demon King held out his hand, lifting it toward Jolynne. Fire came from his fingertips, deep red flames that wound through the air like smoke, curling a path to the pale creature's face. The color was strange against the gray hue of Lucien's colorless world. Fire encircled the faery. Lucien let his power enter her eyes, searching within her for the root of her soul only to find it hidden within her chest, close to her aching heart.

Now that her soul was freely given, his power plucked it easily from the faery. A blessed soul, no matter how battered, was always a powerful delicacy. It fed his magic, strengthened his body and made the blood rush in his veins. His thoughts turned to Mia, even as his demonic eyes burned with a fiery pain. All around them was dark stone lit with bright flames, though their color was still faded.

Lucien drew the flames carrying her soul toward his body. Opening his mouth wide, he swallowed it whole. Pleasure rippled over him, causing him to shiver. His flesh tingled with arousal and he shuddered violently. No matter how many times he did this, no matter how many souls he consumed, each time was like the first. The faery didn't move, but he knew she was still alive and would come to as soon as her body recovered from the shock. She hadn't made a sound while he took it, but inside she'd screamed in pain.

"The fall from grace is always so pleasurable," he said to Anja. The seer giggled. Turning to Nyda, he stepped over her, his feet on either side of her hips. Like all faeries, her outfit barely covered her womanly charms, but though he could appreciate her sexual appeal, his thoughts again turned to the nymph in his bed.

"You should put her back into my care," Anja said.

Realizing that he stared at the ceiling, Lucien snapped his eyes away. When he looked at the soothsayer, she wouldn't meet his gaze.

"I do not—" Nyda began to reject his offer.

"Sh." Lucien fell to his knees, straddling the faery. Placing his palms flat on the floor, he leaned over to hush into her ear. "Nay, blessed one, consider first what I offer. You are a faery lady. A mortal death is not for you. This is not a faery's fate. I see you so frail, so near death, so far from the pretty life you deserve and it saddens my heart. Let me give you pretty things. Give me your burden and I will give you your life back. I can give you the power to take what you want, to have pleasure better than you have ever tasted before because you can have it without consequence."

Nyda turned her head to the side. One of her friends lay crushed and the other unconscious and whole. She swallowed and closed her eyes.

"Death is coming for you. I feel it," Lucien whispered. "It's time to choose."

Nyda opened her eyes, moving her head back toward the Damned King. He pulled the demon from his eyes, letting the fire in them die. Giving her his kindest, most deceiving look, he let a comforting smile cross his mouth. Slowly, she nodded. "Aye. I do not want to die. Take my soul. End the pain."

"I accept." Lucien pushed up, nearly flying to his feet. To Anja and the witch, he said, "Bring forth two of the demons. It is time for them to plant their seeds."

"If you please, my king, I must be sent back to my prison. I feel the Unblessed King will come for me soon," the crone said. "Anja, be a dear and show me the images of the demons mating with the faeries once I'm back in my home. They were always such virile and vicious creatures. I shall enjoy seeing how they take the frail, delicate things."

Lucien lifted his hand, motioning toward the crone to send her back to the Black Palace. "Until we meet again, witch."

The witch bowed her head, before going up in flames. Lucien smiled, breathing hard. His body taut with pent up desire, he willed the demons to hurry. The sooner the mating was over, the sooner he could find his own bed. Tonight, Mia would be his once more.

Chapter Six

"Giants be big and piskies be small, but that no' affect the bedsport at all!" Halton and Gorman sang, their drunken voices ringing high over the Black Palace's great hall. The words slurred into each other, but neither spright seemed to notice in their merriment.

Merrick looked up from his throne, for once not lounging as he sat rigid in waiting. His feet were planted on the floor and his hands gripped tightly together in front of him until both knuckles were white. He frowned at the sprights as they stumbled along the floor, dancing and weaving their way through the watching goblins. He detected liquor on them, even from across the long hall. Drunk, they were obviously unconcerned by the Unblessed King's ill humor.

"Dragons snort fire and sprights do they tame," the two sang in unison.

"With a single glance and a stiff shot of flame," Gorman continued on his own.

Halton frowned, interjecting, "Nay, that's not right. Dragons do not tame sprights. We're renowned for taming dragons. All the realms speak of our prowess as warriors."

"Aye, that's what we said. Sprights snort fire and dragons do they tame." Gorman nodded smartly only to hiccup.

"We snort fire?" Halton asked, his eyes wide in wonderment.

"Of course, we do." Gorman paused, scratching his head thoughtfully. "Though, I have never tried it, have you?"

"Nay." Halton matched his friend's expression.

"Well, there you go." Gorman pointed his finger high into the air in declaration. "We could if we wanted, but—"

"We do not want to." Halton nodded once, pushing out his lower lip.

"Exactly." Gorman drew his finger down with another hiccup.

Merrick cleared his throat, lifting an irritated brow as he got their wandering attention. He'd been waiting for them to get back from Rivershire with his supplies so he could try to call forth the right spell to free his wife from her prison. Finally, he'd sent Bevil and Volos to fetch them and escort them back.

Desperation set in since Juliana scratched her words into his flesh. Had something happened? Was her life in danger? Their child? He felt her rounded stomach and had assumed it was part of his memory. But if she was trapped somewhere other than the stone… He took a deep breath, forcing the worry from his mind. Already the goblins were looking at him curiously. He did not want them feeling his distress.

"Ah, your, ah…" Gorman gulped, swaying on his feet as he looked at Merrick. His wide eyes became even more so.

"Your kingly supreme omni, *hiccup,* presence," Halton filled in, bowing regally at the waist. He waved his hand in circles before him, tapping a foot to keep balance. "We brought your provisions."

Merrick held out his hand, his muscles stiff.

"Ah, right, the supplies," Halton glanced at his friend. "Gorman?"

"Aye?" Gorman asked.

"Give the king his supplies," Halton ordered.

"But you were in charge of acquisitioning the supplies." Gorman tried to smile and meet the Unblessed King's piercing eyes.

"Was not!" Halton growled out of the side of his mouth.

"Was so!" Gorman hissed back.

"Was not!" Halton's voice grew by degrees as he faced Gorman, his fists tight.

"Was—"

"Quiet!" Merrick bellowed, shooting to his feet. "Did you acquire any of what I asked for?"

"Ah." Halton gulped, digging into his pocket. "We have this."

Merrick frowned as the spright ran forward. Halton held up a small stick wand.

"But, that's mine! A muse came to me and said I was to wield it." Gorman gasped, running after his friend in dismay. He tried to hop on Halton's head, but the spright darted to the side at the last minute. Gorman tumbled over, rolling across the floor to land at the king's booted feet.

Merrick leaned down, glaring at him. He waved his hand, building a soundproof wall between them and the goblins on the other side. Now that they had some privacy, he growled, "I will tell my lady wife when she gets back that it was your incompetence that kept her locked away so long in her prison!"

The sprights paled, just as Merrick knew they would. They had bound themselves to his Juliana and being her sprights meant their very happiness was tied to her being pleased with them. They lived to serve the Unblessed Queen and would give their lives for her.

"Take the wand, if it will help." Gorman crawled back on his hands to get away from the king's anger. "But it is not our fault that you do not free her. She told you how."

Halton crawled across the floor, only to lay the wand down by Merrick's feet, pushing it closer with the tip of his long finger, so as not to get too close to the dark elf. He backed up slowly, still on his hands and knees. "If you want her free, you'd free her easily enough. It is not our fault you fight this war."

"This war?" Merrick took a deep breath. He still felt the ache on his chest where Juliana had scratched him. Knowing she was out there, alive and very much aware, ate at him. "What do you mean this war? What do you mean she told me how to free her? She told me nothing."

"She did it to stop the war," Gorman said.

"She hated the fighting. We heard her cry at night when you were away," Halton added. "She worried you would be killed."

Merrick couldn't move.

"She wanted the deaths to stop. She didn't want her baby born feeding off the darker power of the unblessed or feeling death and destruction." Gorman reached a hand out to Halton, who helped him to his feet. They huddled together, backing toward the invisible wall. Pressing their backs against it, they stared wide-eyed at the king.

"She said this?" Merrick smelled their fear and tried to block it.

"She didn't have to," Halton said.

"We are hers and we are loyal to our queen," continued Gorman. "We know her pain. It is our pleasure to help carry the burden of it."

Merrick knew the sprights, being as they were so small and of lesser magic, couldn't carry much of his wife's burden, no matter what it may be.

"Already we say too much," Gorman said.

"We will not betray her," Halton added.

"You know how to free her, don't you?" Merrick forced himself to be calm. If he continued to yell, like he wanted, the two sprights wouldn't tell him anything. If he was calm, if he didn't strike them until they were bloody masses on his main hall floor, they would tell him what he needed to know.

"Aye," Gorman said.

Halton slapped his palm over the other spright's mouth as if to quiet him, even as he said, "She left you a missive. You know as well as we."

"Missive? What missive?" Merrick had searched the entire castle for word from her.

"With your witch," Gorman whispered. "The evil one that lives in the darkness. She came from the bowels of the palace to help Juliana. We dare not speak to her, but the queen did. They talked softly and fast as we hid around the corner."

"The witch?" Merrick felt sick to his stomach. The crone he kept locked in the dungeon had been set free to help Juliana? He hoped the sprights were wrong. The witch could not be trusted.

Throwing his senses out over his palace, he felt her evil presence still locked away where he kept her imprisoned. It had been a long while since he went to her for help, for doing so came with a heavy price. He'd used her powers to save Sir

Thomas' life, bringing him back from the dead. The deed had cost him two drops of his own powerful blood and a promise that almost caused him to lose his wife. But when he'd asked her for help to locate Juliana's brothers, she'd refused, saying she got more pleasure out of his misery, for he'd have to tell Juliana that he couldn't find the Bellemare men.

Juliana's brothers were now safe, their lives never really having been in as great of peril as he'd thought at the time. Had the witch been talking about something else? What had she said exactly?

I get more from not helping with this—much amusement.

She'd been talking about Juliana's brothers, but perhaps she meant his whole situation.

Oooh, broken, the witch had said about his heart when she had tried to speak of Juliana to him.

She'd been enjoying his pain. The evil harpy belonged more to Lucien's magic, the power of complete and utter darkness, but for Merrick to release her from her prison would be to send her back to the side of evil. Doing so wasn't an option. Evil had enough power as it was. So he kept her locked away where she could do little harm.

"The witch," he whispered, gritting his teeth as he thought of the old woman touching his wife. His body instantly dissolved into mist as he drifted out of his hall to a small crack in the floor. It was a place only his magic could pass through. If Juliana, in having his power, somehow found a way to change the prisons below, who knew what kind of madness she could have unleashed on the world. The witch was bad, but by no means the worst.

Going to the deepest pits of the castle, the Unblessed King solidified, standing near his dungeons. The curved ceilings of the passageways were low and he ducked his head under the arched doorways. The place felt the same, for all of Juliana's tampering with it, but he couldn't help the bit of anger that arose as he thought of his wife scheming with the witch. If she rearranged his castle enough to let the crone out, she could have released any matter of evil into the world. The few prisoners he did keep locked behind his walls had been there since before he'd become king and were too insane to be set free. They were to remain where they were for all eternity.

"I warned her of this," he fumed quietly, before summonsing the small, portly goblin who served as the prisoner's caretaker. "Werdan!"

Almost instantly, the goblin wobbled leisurely around a dim, stone corner. Without breaking his pace, he came along the passageway. His eyes were completely white, unseeing in the way other creatures knew. Instead, Werdan felt the walls and sensed the prisoners. The goblin knew every brick and stone by heart.

"My king?" the caretaker inquired, shuffling to a stop before him.

"Account for all the prisoners."

The goblin's white eyes glowed, swirling with dark rings of smoke before clearing. "All here. Only the witch's power shifts."

"More than usual?"

"Nay, not so much more." Werdan's gruff tone rasped over each word.

Merrick strode past the caretaker, toward the far end of the passageway. He didn't bother to knock against the metal door before slamming the flat of his hand against it. A loud whine sounded over the hall before metal crashed against stone. His gaze instantly searched the round chamber, half expecting the old crone to be gone.

The large brick walls were overgrown with moss. The witch had lived beneath the castle for centuries, surviving in her little round room of magic. Broken bottles littered the hearth. A stone ledge wound around the walls, filled with jars of herbs and vials of other mystical concoctions.

In the center on a raised stone pedestal sat the witch. Her gown was pretty, sparkling abnormally in the candle glow. She turned her wrinkled face toward the door, sniffing in his direction. He took a deep breath, not stepping into the room as he waited for her to speak.

"My king." The old woman's tone was frailer than he knew her to be. "What honor is this after so long that you deign to grace this tiny dwelling? Or have you a need of my services?"

Merrick wasn't surprised that she knew who was in her doorway. In her blindness, she saw many things. Though she could not be trusted completely, she was very powerful and worth keeping around—not that he could kill her if he wanted to.

"Anger replaces the pain," the witch said. "Have you finally discovered more of the truth? I daresay it took you long enough, for I expected this visit long before now."

"Then give me what I seek and be done with your games," Merrick ordered. He resisted the urge to beat the woman. It would do no good, she'd only enjoy it.

"Tell me what you seek and I shall give whatever I can." The witch slowly pushed to her feet, shuffling toward the herb-filled ledge.

"End the spell that traps my wife in stone," he ordered.

"Is the queen in stone?" The woman smacked her lips, only to cackle.

"End the spell," he enunciated. "At once."

"I cannot end it," she laughed, "only you can do that, my king, and I'm afraid you no longer have the means. It is too late. You waited too long to discover the truth."

"How did you do it? How did you trap her?"

"You did it, my king. It was your blood that cast the spell. And she did it. Queen Juliana's will bound the magic." She again cackled, the hard, grating tone echoing over the hall. "You traded your blood to me for the life of Sir Thomas the Mortal and now that blood payment has sent your wife running away."

"Give me the missive," Merrick stepped inside the room, feeling a dark chill wash over him by crossing the short distance. He detected power—old, evil power. Lucien. A thin barrier trapped her in her prison. It was why there was no lock on her door. But the barrier also locked her magic in.

"Missive?" the witch asked, her voice tight.

"Now!" Merrick's voice darkened. "Give me the missive from my wife!"

"Mm," she moaned in pleasure, lifting her hands with palms toward him. "Or what? You will shower me with more of your anger and pain? Both equally as sweet. Will you set me afire like a naughty goblin in your hall? Banish me from the palace like an impudent warrior?"

"Nay," Merrick walked toward her. Gripping her bony face, he squeezed hard. She began to smile at the rough hold, until his words stopped the joyous expression. "I'll give you to my brother, King Ean. You'll be in a pretty dungeon in the Golden Palace at Tegwen, living in ugly rags, surrounded by pleasure and love for all eternity."

For the first time since he'd known her, the witch appeared shaken. She stumbled back, pressed into the circular wall.

"Should I summons the Blessed King?" Merrick motioned as if he would go. "He would be bound by duty to take you from me."

"Nay, but I cannot give you the missive," the witch said. "I destroyed it."

"What did it say?" Even as he asked, he knew he had no wish to hear Juliana's words spoken by the horrible woman. It turned his stomach even to know his wife had been in the crone's presence. Being more specific, he asked, "How do I break the spell?"

"I will tell you if you give me your word as king you will not send me to the Golden Palace for speaking it."

"Fine." Merrick crossed his arms over his chest, waiting. "But it better work."

"Only the blood of brothers will free her, given willingly."

"I have to get the blood of William, Hugh and Thomas?" That wouldn't be too difficult of a task. Her brothers would freely give their blood to help her. It was no secret that Juliana loved her family. Did she do this to get them together? "Easily done."

"Nay, the blood of royal brothers on opposing thrones." The witch's cackle again rang over him. "You must make peace with King Ean and use his blood with your own to free your wife. She feels the bond between you and King Ean and thinks to mend it so as to end your pain. The curse is until both blessed and unblessed royal blood unites to free her. If you do not join with Ean, she will be lost for all eternity. Or until two more such brothers sit on the two thrones."

Such a thing was a near impossibility. Two brothers, one king of the unblessed and the other of the blessed? The seats of power did not turn over so quickly. Then, there was the fact they were at war. Ean owed him nothing. Why would he help him free the Unblessed Queen? The last time he saw his brother, he'd said some very cruel things. Ean would not trust him enough to help him. There might be one way, one thing he knew for sure Ean would want besides possible peace. Mayhap, he could promise him to free Wolfe or die trying. Merrick glared at the old woman, willing her to continue.

"There is more," the crone said. "The ritual has to be done with Queen Juliana's jeweled dagger. The one given to her in love from her family."

Lucien had Juliana's dagger. Hugh had seen it. "You gave her dagger to the Damned King."

"Me?" she shook her head. "How could I? I am locked away here in the dungeon."

"Juliana let you out and you discovered a way to escape. That is how you got the new gown you wear. I smell the Damned King all over you."

The woman didn't move. Merrick could detect a trace of her fear, calling his power. He began to feed off her, growing stronger as she grew weaker, though she tried to appear brave.

"You've been very wicked, haven't you, crone?"

"I'm inherently evil." She gave a feeble laugh. "Is it really a surprise?"

"If my wife and child don't come back unharmed, you will be inherently trapped in the happiest place I can find. I'm talking children and laughing and true love, eternal happy."

"I should not be punished for the actions of Queen Juliana," her voice dropped to a whine, "for who am I to question the order of the Unblessed Queen?"

Merrick arched a brow, not believing her act of loyal servitude.

"There is nothing I can do." The witch's tone hardened once more. "I told you how to break the queen's spell. If she dies, the fault will be yours. Not mine. And if you dare to punish me for it, consequences will be had."

"Aye, consequences." Merrick nodded, letting his eyes fill in black. "For without my wife, you will face happy consequences indeed."

Merrick lifted his hand, stripping her of her pretty new gown. She screeched in irritation. "Stop taking my gowns! Is that all you can do, high king? Steal an old woman's clothing?"

"You enjoy my misery, witch," Merrick said as he strode away from the naked woman huddling on the floor, "and I shall enjoy yours."

Chapter Seven

Mystic Forest, Kingdom of Hades Border

King Ean felt the heat of the Fire Palace, even from his distance in the forest. Though he wanted to, he didn't dare go any closer. Lucien would feel him the moment he entered Hades and, magical cloak or not, they would lose their only chance at freeing Wolfe from the dungeons.

The war had not spread into this part of the forest. Along the borders to Hades, the trees did not thrive. The trunks seemed to choke on ash, the leaves pale and gray. Animals did not come there willingly lest they be devoured by the demons who lived within the woods—terrifying man-beasts who turned to uncontrollable, bloodlusting wolves nightly with the passing of the silver moon.

"We should hurry. I don't want to be caught here when the lycanthropes rise," Adal said, as if reading Ean's thoughts. Behind them the unicorns pawed the ground. They'd been uneasy, their anxiety growing with each closer step. He did not want to bring the majestic creatures and knew, if it came to losing them to Lucien, he would order them all killed first. The unicorns were there because of their quick flight of foot and the magical senses that would warn them before danger arrived.

Hitting the side of his leg in frustration, Ean answered, "I want to go with you. It should be my life at risk."

Adal nodded, understanding. "Tegwen will go on without a commander and guards. It will not fair so well without a king. You know as well as I that Prince Ladon is not fit to take the throne in your absence. He cannot even bring himself to come back to this realm. Who knows what condition Wolfe is in, should he be freed."

"He will be freed," Ean said, confidently, though he did not feel so certain.

"Aye, when he is freed," Adal amended. By the look in the commander's eyes, he did not feel the confidence of his words either.

Two other elves were with them. Levin would stay with Ean in the forest as guard for he had the best hearing and was light of foot when it came to running. Brodor the Bravehearted, an old, wise warrior who had been in more battles than any elf Ean knew, would venture into the Fire Palace with Adal. They all knew the risks of such an undertaking. Death was almost certain, detection and imprisonment even more so. But now that he found a way in, how could Ean not take it?

"The wizard assured me this would work." Ean reached into his tunic, pulling out a bound leather satchel. Though small, it was filled with great magic.

"Are you sure he can be trusted? Only a dark wizard could find his way in." Adal hesitated before taking the magic.

"Because only a dark wizard could get in, is why we must deal with a dark wizard. Lucky for us, Geraint Aldred's interests lie with our own." Ean glanced at Brodor, who listened without appearing to. His long beard distinguished him from the other elfin guard. He did not take to fashion, having lived for so long the man did not give credence to such things. "He and his order of wizards are upset with the Unblessed King for rearranging the realm at will and interfering with their balance. Dark or light, all wizards want balance. Their magic depends upon it. They see our freeing Wolfe as a chance to strike back at Merrick who has been searching as ardently as I for a way to free our brother."

"If death comes this hour, it is as good a time as any other," Brodor said gruffly, slipping his sword into a lambskin sheath. The dark brown of his clothing blended with the surrounding forest, making him nigh impossible to see from a distance. "I am ready."

Levin looked as if he wanted to say something equally as brave, but swallowed his words in the presence of the greater warrior. He merely nodded, turning his attention to the quiver of arrows he carried.

CRROED

Lucien's eyes lit with a combination of pleasure and arousal. His own shaft was hard from watching the erotically brutal show taking place in his hall. He'd summonsed two altars to appear on his main hall floor, a hard bed in view of all who watched. But the Demon King wasn't the only one whose desires were awakened.

Six mortal high priests chanted their dark and droning tones, adding atmospheric music as they set the thrusting pace of the daimons with the rise and fall of their voices. Beneath the red and black robes, their members were thick with sexual excitement. A few of the men had brought handmaids with them, pretty human slaves they forced beneath their robes to suck their shafts between warm lips. Only the women's toes poked out. The great folds of material hid the rest of their naked bodies. Others stroked themselves, jealously watching the two daimons with their faery brides, eager for a chance to be called forth for a chance to claim the delicate beings when the daimons had planted their seeds. Whichever of them were chosen to take the pregnant women back would be able to seek their pleasure in them however they liked. Not that the faeries would mind, their own echoes of soulless pleasure carried over the chants.

Not to be outdone, six dark priestesses lifted their voices, urging the couples on. Their hips thrust in time, as they searched the crowd of demons who'd come to bear witness. One even stared at Lucien, her dark eyes begging him to call to her, to use her, to let her use him. She had a beautiful mouth and Lucien thought of letting her step forward to his throne. Thoughts of the nymph kept him from doing so.

Lucien tapped his fingers, letting his nails fall in rhythm against the arm of his throne. A great heat came from the center fire pit, illuminating the altars. Lucien slowly let his eyes roam past them to the hideous faces of his demon subjects. Some had gnarled bodies, ravaged by time and hate. Others were like corpses, their rotting flesh peeled off their bones. Even a clan of hairy lycanthropes had come from their home in the forest, fangs bared, to watch.

The darkness he saw in his subjects fueled him. These demons were the purest breeds, spawned from devil pacts and torn from between the thighs of their mothers as creatures of darkness. Never having known a soul, they were not torn in their purpose, did not feel regret or guilt. And there was no hiding what they were, not like half demons or the possessed that appeared like another race only to hide the truth inside where none could see. That was one of the reasons they would all sire or carry children to create his demon army of half-breeds, born without souls but able to hide their evil within innocent faces.

Thinking of such deceit, he detected Anja in the prisons, pouting that she was not allowed to come up and watch. He'd grown tired of her insolence over Mia and banished her down into the pits. Lucien almost felt sorry for the prisoners he kept there as the soothsayer took her pouting rage out on them.

Then, in the center taking their claim of the faeries, were the daimons—demons with flesh as red as blood and eyes as black as night. Justly feared, the daimons possessed the greatest power, the utmost hate and a brazen appetite for destruction. They were unstoppable once they set to a course, so long as they had the means to fulfill it. Their only weakness was that they were trapped in the evil fires of his palace. They could not live in the immortal realm for long before being called back and, like Lucien, they could never travel to the mortal world—none of the pure demons could unless they attached themselves to the soul of a mortal. The daimon couldn't attach to a soul, for to touch a soul would be to kill it instantly

The only one not finding pleasure in the entertainment was Sir Nicholas, whose vacant eyes stared on as calm as watching a butterfly attack and as unmoved as a boulder. He was truly dead, his body moving without much purpose, his mind shut off to all but what he was ordered to do. Seeing a priestess eyeing Nicholas, Lucien knew the man had caught her eye and would be ordered to do much once the daimons finished.

The chanting crescendoed into a scream of moans and release. Already Lucien could tell the daimons' seed had taken hold in the faeries' wombs, even before their lovers pulled their hard, bruising lengths from within the delicate bodies.

Almost instantly, an orgy of flesh ensued. A priestess grabbed Sir Nicholas, tugging him with her to the floor. The man didn't fight her. A lycan woman grabbed a priest, clawing his handmaid away from him before riding him to the floor. The stunned woman only had a moment to catch her breath before

113

the lycan's brother claimed her for his own. She screamed, but her fear only added flames to the raging sexual fire in the hall.

Lucien didn't stay to watch as he surged through the hall in a streak of flames, leaving the orgy behind him. Abovestairs, waiting for him in his bed, was Mia. So long he'd been without her, as she stayed locked in his prison and then to have to wait as he took care of the duties of his kingdom. The faeries' souls still empowered him, even as the carnal performance in his hall flamed his lusts.

As he moved, the scorched bricks of the hall righted themselves, becoming brighter. The worn tapestries fluttered, ridding themselves of ash and dust, the threads winding over the holes to repair old wounds, until they hung in black glory once more. Crumbled statues rolled to sudden demon grace, the figures flawlessly mended. Today was a good day for the Demon King. His subjects were pleased and busy. Mia was back in his bed. Souls fed his dark power with a rush of energy. And King Ean's men were approaching his castle in an effort to free Prince Wolfe, unaware that he orchestrated everything the loyal high wizard, Geraint Aldred, told them.

He solidified from the flames, pushing the demon back into his flesh. The demon in him liked to play, but Lucien knew Mia preferred the man. As he stepped into the bedchamber, he could not pull the flames from within his dark eyes. Fire grew in his palms a roaring ball he drew together out of old habit, rolling and bouncing it in his palm.

His palace continued to right itself, the stone walls healing, the long sheer material cleaning themselves into inky perfection as they fluttered from the ceiling in long columns. The strips drew to the side, forming a path from the door to the bed. Within the fireplace, the flames died from orange to blue, darkening the chamber while still giving it light. The basins, candles and torches did the same, darkening in smokeless

114

perfection. He pulled the fireball he carried into his fist, smiting it. When he opened his hand, a little puff of smoke was all that was left.

As the palace change grew forward toward the bed, creeping up the sides to where Mia rested, he watched as his will caused the material of her tattered gown to change. The bodice blackened from grayed white, tightening around her breasts. Unlike outfits he'd given her in the past, this one was soft, covering her completely. A deep V formed over her chest, held up by narrow straps. Dirt and grime, ash and coal, all disappeared, leaving her flesh pale and clean. Bruises on her ankles and wrists healed, dried blood disappeared.

As the gown formed, its skirt flowed down over her legs like a mortal woman's, only more beautiful. Lighter gray showed along the split front, forming to her still legs. The gray spread upward over the bodice, sewing itself in thin winding patterns. Her head was turned, but as her hair lifted, curling around the crown of her head, her sleep-tinted cheeks were revealed, as was the long line of her perfect neck. The pulse beating in her throat captured his notice. Dark kohl drew along her eyes, matching the color spreading over her lush mouth. Her lips parted in breath.

The boots disappeared from his feet, leaving them bare like he preferred, and his own long tunic changed to match hers. He blocked the sounds of the hall below, not wanting to hear the demons, not now, not when he was with her.

The walls began to crystallize, sparkling like tiny diamonds in the stone. Lucien didn't touch her, as he took the spell off her, letting her awaken. Fire streamed along his fingertips, winding down over her. He could feel her as the flame trails moved, but it wasn't as intimate as physical touch, flesh to flesh.

Lashes fluttered, sweeping up. Lucien waited, letting the fire skim up her body like a soaring falcon. It caressed her cheek, turning her face toward him. Blinking once, violet eyes met his. Thin black threads marred their perfection, only to be hidden in the round orbs as they cleared.

For the briefest of moments, he caught his reflection in her gaze. A hint of ash still marred him around his eyes, darkening the skin around the black orbs. His hair hung down around his face, long, straight black locks that reached his waist. She blinked and the image was gone as a hint of tears watered her eyes.

"Mia," he whispered, unable to say aught but that one word as he waited for her to speak.

"Do not call me that," she whispered, her voice hoarse. "Mia was a happy, carefree nymph who knew naught of sin. I am not Mia. I am something else."

Lucien should have been heartened by her words, but he couldn't be. He sensed a part of her had died while down in his dungeons. He did it to her, sent her there, kept her there, and yet he wished there could have been another way. "What should I call you then, sinful nymph? Mianthros?"

"Mia is Mianthros. My mother blessed me with that name. As I told you when I first came here, you do not get to use it."

"Then what?" Lucien retracted the flames into his hand, but didn't move otherwise.

"You decide. You decide everything else for me. You even ordered I not be harmed. Anja would not have left me untouched had you not told her to. I would thank you, but I know enough of you to understand, if you did tell her to leave me be, you had your dark reason for doing so. It was not because you cared what happened. You do not care about anything. You cannot."

"How harsh you judge." He didn't like what he felt as she said the words. His first reaction was to lash out, but he held back. This wasn't the reaction he'd expected from her, though he wasn't exactly sure what it was he did expect. Gratitude for freeing her, mayhap? Or anger that he left her down there so long? Whatever it was, this quiet deadness inside her wasn't it. He wanted the fire back in her eyes. He wanted the resistance.

"Offense does not suit you, Lucien. Stop pretending to care." She took a deep breath. "Mia's dead. I don't know what I am, but it's not her. You win, Lucien. I'm done fighting."

"Are you pouting?" He forced a cruel, short laugh, trying to rile her spirits. "Oh, nymph, do you mourn your William so much? You should have left with him. Do not blame me because you did not fight for your freedom."

She gave a weak laugh. "I should have known you saw that."

"I see everything." His mind turned to outside his castle. King Ean's men were close. He left the way unguarded. Let them slip inside his palace.

"What point is there in running?" Her gaze was steady on his. "You would have summonsed me back. You possess my soul, remember?"

"And you bartered it to me freely, if you will remember." His eyes flamed in irritation. This was not how he expected her to awaken. His body tight, he wanted to throw himself on top of her—punish her, torture her, feel her.

"You were supposed to kill me, Lucien. I bartered my soul and you were to take all of it from me, but instead you took half and left me with feeling. Had I known that is what you planned, I would have killed myself instead. I would kill myself still, but for the fact you'd bring me back."

Angry, he shot forward. His fingers digging into the soft bed he'd created for her, holding her down by her hair as his hands rested on the sides of her head. Violet eyes stared up at him, unafraid, unemotional. His knees pressed along the outside of her thighs, trapping her legs with the gown he'd given her. Curling his lips, he glared, wanting her fear, needing it.

"Go ahead." She laughed, the sound on the brink of insanity. She didn't fight him, not with her body, not with her eyes. "End me. End this game. Do it."

His breath left him in a long, ugly hiss. "A new game, is it? And what rules apply this time, my mistress?"

"I never asked to be your mistress, Lucien."

"I did not wait for you to give your permission."

"There is no game. I am done. You have used me up." She tried to look away, but his hold on her hair kept her head where it was. "End it, Lucien. It's over between us. I am done. Or give me a knife so that I may end myself."

Lucien pulled back, his legs straddling her thighs. Lifting his hand beside his head, flames erupted to form Lady Juliana's jeweled dagger. Mia flinched, but didn't move to stop him. With one thrust he could stab down, ending the beat of her heart like she pleaded with him to do. The small thread of fear in her was overwhelmed by the hope. She wanted him to do it, wanted to be murdered. Her arms stirred, sliding up along the bed so her body formed into a cross. She closed her eyes, nodding for him to do it.

"The Blessed King's men enter the palace to free Prince Wolfe from my dungeon," he whispered. Her eyes opened. Lucien gave a small smile.

Ah, there is the fire. Not quite as dead as you would have it, sweet nymph.

"King Ean himself waits in the forest. He thinks I can't detect him, but you see, I knew he would come. It was my wizard who told him how to free Wolfe. He walks into a trap." Lucien's eyes filled completely black, purposefully piquing her interest in his words. She trembled and turned her head sharply away. "I'm going to kill him. I'm going to end the Blessed King. Even now the lycanthropes feast in my hall, awaiting my command. They're going to hunt him down and kill him. The Blessed throne will be empty. Wolfe will not survive the escape, Merrick has a throne and Ladon is unfit to rule."

"I do not care to hear this." The words were calm, but they were also a lie.

"Nay?" Lucien chuckled. "Should I kill you then?"

She nodded and her muscles tightened, not so confident as before.

He began to stab down. Mia gasped, closing her eyes tight. Lucien stopped, the blade tip against the exposed valley of her breasts. A single drop of blood formed when she took a deep breath, her skin pressing up toward the blade. Slowly her eyes opened, glancing first at the stayed knife and then to him. Lucien pulled it back, swinging the dagger in his hand to offer her the hilt. "Actually, methinks I would rather see you do it."

Her hand shook as she took the hilt, angling it so she could stab inward at her chest. Lucien circled his hips and reached to the skirt along her waist. Pulling it, he willed the material to glide beneath his knees. She glanced down, as if surprised by the act.

"What do you care?" he whispered. "You have already decided to be dead. I only wish to feel the death throes while inside you." His clothing disappeared, leaving him naked as he bunched the skirt at her waist. He would call her bluff. "Which would you prefer? The demon or the man?"

"They are the same, Lucien. Two faces for the same being. All demon."

Lucien knew that wasn't true, even if she did believe it. But why correct her mistake? She would believe what she wanted to. Letting the fire enter his gaze, the control he had over the beast slipped. Ashen flesh grew around the dark pits of his eyes. Fangs and claws stretched out, pointing, eager for blood. "Then I won't bother to hide the beast."

Arousal towered the mass between his thighs. Desire hummed, his blood impassioned with the need to feel her again. Too long it had been since he'd taken her and the urgency was only fueled by the demon orgy he'd witnessed in the hall, the faery souls he'd dined on. Almost roughly he lifted his knees and pushed her thighs open.

His nymph gasped. Fire came from his shaft, reaching toward her sex. The orange flames narrowed around her clit, heating it without burning, roaring around the bud until it was so sensitive she jerked. Sweat beaded on her flesh and the grip on the knife weakened but didn't let go.

"Ah, ah," she panted, her voice lost in the breath.

"Beg me to let King Ean live." Lucien drew his hips closer.

"If you kill him, ah, the war will end." She spread her legs wider.

Lucien grinned. She did still care. "You are not as broken as you pretend to be."

"Aren't you going to chain me? Make me beg?"

"Nay, I'm going to prove to you that you want to be here, despite what you know to be right and good. I'm going to make you respond to me, love me, beg for me. Succumb to me completely and willingly, sweet nymph. You are damned. Nothing you do can take the blackness from your soul, not even death." He drew the fire from her sex. His erection was painful, stretching the limits of his flesh and it would only continue to grow as the beast clawed its way to his surface. "Show me how much you need me. Pull me into you."

"I hate you." The words lacked venom, but for the first time he felt she might truly mean them. It wasn't like the times she'd said it in the past, hating herself because she dared to feel love for him.

The chamber was hot, but the heat didn't bother his chilled flesh. Fire did not burn him. Love did not affect him. Duty did not chain him, not in the ways it did other men. But her hatred, the hint of it, wounded him more than he would ever tell her.

"You do not mean..." For once his confidence was shaken. Lying, he said, "I smell your love for me. It's why you hate yourself."

"I used to look into your eyes, Lucien, and think I'd catch glimpses of something redeemable, no matter how small a part of you it was." Even as she spoke, her legs stirred in bodily desire. "I used to tell myself there was something in you worth caring for. It was the only way I could stand existing as your slave. It was the only way I could forgive myself for succumbing. But there is nothing redeemable in you, is there? There is nothing worth loving. At most, you are a shell of something that once was, long ago, the man before the beast consumed it. Just like King Ean was an elf before being King of the Blessed. Just as Merrick was before being Unblessed. You started as something else, a non-demonic being. But all real traces of whatever creature that was, are gone now, Lucien. You are a shell controlled by a pure demon. If you feel anything, it's only your vanity being affronted."

He merely stared at her, his naked body poised for entrance, as he waited for her to accept him willingly, to draw his hips forward.

"It's the way magic works, isn't it?" she continued, her hands at her sides, not reaching for him as she had in the past. All damnation for herself was gone, all self-hatred. "You are the demon. You are the pure one who put the dead Lucien shell on to rule, mimicking emotion and feelings when you have none. You were the shell because it allowed you to exist in the realms. You are the thing, the nothingness, the pure evil feeding on the emotions and dark deeds that will forever burn regardless of the shell that carries you."

She was wrong. He did feel, though not as one with a soul did. He wanted things, desired them, craved them. Part of the man he'd been lingered still and what he carried couldn't even be called a real demon. Although it was the easiest way to describe what he kept leashed, what he carried was more than a demon. It was the darkest magic. The evil was because everything else was and it needed someone to carry it.

And, yet, she was right as well, for he did feed on the dark deeds, dark emotions. For that reason, he could not have a soul. It would burn up in an instant should he even try to possess one.

"Believing you still carried a man inside you made it hard for me to hate you, but now, understanding and accepting that there is nothing more than a shell filled with evil, allows me to. I needed to think there was a man inside the darkness—a man worthy of love, one I could care for. But, it was a lie. I know you feel nothing either way, only get pleasure and power from my torment. So, my Demon King, I finally accept. You are what you are and you will feed off my self-hatred no longer. Take my broken soul and be done with it."

"What do you want from me? A declaration of love?" He laughed, shaking his head. "Do you think this pretty speech of yours will spill flowery passions from me? Or do you think I will beg you to love me?"

122

"I already said I know you—"

His look cut her off, for suddenly he felt it, the thing she was trying hard to hide, to kill. A small glimmer of a feeling she carried for him still, the tiny piece of her self-hate because of it. Leaning toward her, his mouth hovering near hers, he said, "I will never release you."

Lucien pressed his mouth to hers, grinding his sharpened teeth along her mouth until he tasted blood—their blood, mingling together as she accepted his harsh embrace. He captured her moans with his lips, swallowing them as she gave in. Soft, warm hands ran up his arms, only to glide down his sides. For once, as they came together, it was only the two of them—mistress and Demon King. There were no chains, no knives except for the Unblessed Queen's jeweled dagger she'd left discarded beside them.

Her hands slid along his sides, even as her legs parted wide. She pulled his hips, leading his shaft to her soft folds. Lucien growled in the back of his throat as he felt the wet heat inviting him closer. Her shortened nails clawed the cheeks of his ass and he willed those nails to grow so they bit into his flesh, drawing blood. He resisted entering as she forced him forward, his muscles flexing into tight bunches. Lucien wanted her to beg for it.

"Lucien, please," she begged, mindlessly lifting her hips to his. "Please."

"Tell me you love me. Let me hear the words."

"I love you," she mouthed, a tear streaming over her cheek. "Damn you, I love you."

Lucien thrust, a loud cry echoing off his lips. He didn't care who heard his animalistic growls. The sound from the hall below, of fornication and pleasure echoed around them as he let them in. Grunts sounded, propelling his hips forward until she was stretched wide to take him all.

He clawed at her gown, ripping it from her in hard slashes. A breast spilled forward between the gashed material. Grabbing it, he squeezed, letting fire heat his palm as the nipple budded against his flesh. Incensed with arousal, he thrust harder, pounding forward violently. His fangs strained.

"Beg me to drink," he ordered.

She tossed her head to the side, offering it to him. Softly, she panted, "Aye."

Lucien bared his fangs, biting down on her neck. The taste of blood flowed freely into him and he swallowed in deep satisfaction. His member expanded inside her as the beast was unleashed. She moaned, her body tense as release finally came over her. He let her have it, not keeping her from the edge as he'd done often in the past. Pulling his crimson-stained mouth from her bloody neck, his eyes flashed with power as he healed the wound. He continued to pump until he too exploded, releasing his seed inside her.

Breathing hard, he fell to the side. The dagger poked him in the back, but he didn't care. "Arice. I rename you Arice."

She glanced at him, not showing pleasure as he granted her wish for a new name.

"You are my Ari." Lucien couldn't stop himself from touching her cheek. "Mia is dead, as you wish. Your blessed past is no more. Now can you accept this life?"

Ari didn't answer.

"I have guests to attend and the blessed guards are nearing Wolfe's prison. You sleep. I will come back when my plans for King Ean are finished so that we may baptize you into this world properly." Lucien stood, a dark long tunic and tight breeches forming over him as he moved. His bare feet hit upon the stone as he walked through the parted gauze toward the door. He felt lighter, relaxed.

"I'm tired of hating myself," she whispered behind him. He began to smile, only to stiffen as a sickening gasp sounded over the unmistakable stabbing of a blade. He turned in time to see her hand falling from the jeweled dagger. His expression fell. She'd killed herself.

Violet eyes, the life ebbing out of them, stared blankly at him. Instantly, he lifted his hand, forcing the last thread of her life, her soul, to stay where it was. She jerked several times as he kept her alive, blood streaming from her parted lips. He held her in the pain, even as he rushed to her side to stop it.

"You are mine," he growled in anger, the beast consuming his features. He reached for the blade, jerking it out of her. Warm, sticky blood ran over his hand. "You are mine, even more as all remnants of Mia die at your own hands, Ari. But I will not take all of her soul. I let you keep half so that you may continue to feel. For if I cannot feel as you have said, then I will watch you feel for me. There is no escape for you, Ari. You are the Damned King's mistress. You have not past, not future, only this. You will be worshiped for all eternity by demons. Like it or not, you are now a part of the darkness."

She closed her eyes, crying as she shook her head in denial. He stood again, taking the knife with him this time as he left her where she was—bloody and torn. With a wave of his hand, chains came up from the bed, locking her in place so she couldn't do herself harm.

"I told you once in another life and I'll tell you once more in this new one," Lucien said as he paused by the door. "I can give you everything or I can take it all away. The choice is yours, Ari. Believe me when I say, death is not the worst I am capable of."

Chapter Eight

For once, Juliana did not hope that Merrick called her back to be with him. She missed him, missed his touch, but the Black Palace was becoming too dangerous. The spirits that haunted the stone halls grew in number and with each passing second they became bolder, reaching for her from their dark shadows with their rotting corpse hands. Their cruel hisses lifted over the hall, louder until they practically howled.

"Unwanted. Unloved."

"Forgotten bride."

"Death to the queen."

"He doesn't want you. Never wanted you. Join us."

"Death is the only escape."

Thinking of it made her walk faster through the stone forest. Her side ached, but at least the baby rested within her belly. The clack of her feet on the hard ground sounded over the silence, punctuated only by the occasional leaves breaking as she brushed against them. They fell hard to the ground.

Behind her was the palace, and towering above that the mountains. The gray and charcoal landscape sparkled in the silvery moonlight. She was used to darkness following her almost anywhere she went, but there were strange periods of dawn and sunset that seemed to break the darkness, though the sun never shone as bright as it had over her childhood home.

She hesitated, unsure if she should try to find Lord Kalen in the mountains where he lived, not that she knew where that was, or if she should wander the forest in search of the battlefront. With his psychic powers, he was the only one she knew of that could help her now. If Kalen couldn't hear her, then she might really be trapped.

Though doubt did plague her, Juliana tried not to succumb. Merrick would not have let her and their child slide into a dangerous world. Mayhap this was all her fault. Mayhap his witch, with his droplets of blood, could not be trusted.

Above her, frozen in the sky, a flock of birds was suspended, their light blue a strange contrast to the normal gray. A squirrel sat unmoving in a tree, looking to eternally chew on a nut. Every detail of his small hands was carved to perfection, even the fur sticking up from his back. Suddenly, one of the boulders on the other side of the path began to move. A boulder next to a tree was suspiciously like a hiding chubby woodland gnome. Next to the rock sat a squat little man with round red cheeks, tiny features, a hat, jacket and a beard long enough to touch the ground.

"Your mother is a fool, little one," she whispered, rubbing her stomach. "I was so overwhelmed with the unblessed magic, I acted in what methought to be the only way. Instead, I should have talked to your father, pleaded with him, denied him, whatever it took to end the war. I should have been stronger. I'm sorry if I failed us. I wanted nothing more than to see you born, to see your face, to see you happy and safe."

A giggle sounded. Juliana tensed, looking up into the stone forest. The laugh rang out, louder than before. It was a child, a girl.

"Ho! Who's there?" Juliana trembled, nervous. She wasn't scared, not of a child's voice, but her baby hadn't kicked for a long while and now, as she desperately wanted to see it, she heard beautiful laughter. Though she hoped for her child, she was anxious to see another face—a real live, solid person. Footsteps sounded over the forest floor and she moved to follow them. The laughter was her only answer, an impish giggling that rang so sweet it made Juliana's heart ache. "Where are you? Please, show yourself."

"You are new to the forest."

Juliana turned, gasping as the sound came from behind. The voice belonged to a delicate wisp of girl with long blonde hair and soulful blue eyes. Her heart nearly stopped beating to see it and she imagined that the eyes could very well be Bellemare eyes, the hair could be from Merrick's blessed side. The child smiled and curtseyed, gently lifting the skirt of her dark blue tunic gown. It was cut in the mortal style, just as Juliana would make for her own daughter.

"Where did you come from?" Juliana asked, shaking. "Who are you?"

The child's eyes moved briefly to her stomach. Juliana's hand followed the gaze, resting on her still baby. She'd been alone for so long, to see this child now made her ache and hope. Feeling a strange softness, she glanced down. Her own gown had changed, matching the blue the child wore. The linen was unlike any she'd ever felt, as soft as fur yet the fibers were short. The material was so light it was like air against her skin. The skirt split down the front, the blue pooling to the sides of her belly as cream linen was exposed down the front.

"I've come to guide you, my lost lady." The child turned, skipping into the trees. "I've come to take you home. You cannot stay here in the stone. The spirits know you are here and you do not belong. They will hunt you if you do not leave."

Juliana hurried to follow her, thinking of the dark spirits that swam through the Black Palace, the same that chased her out into the forest in search of Lord Kalen. "Wait. Who are you?"

"I have come to lead you from the stone. I have come to show you the way out. There is only one way, one chance. Come with me. It is time to leave this place. Life waits for you on the other side."

Juliana followed the girl, desperate to believe. What other choice did she have? To not follow? To wander the forest alone for all eternity? To stay and be chased by the evil spirits that hunted her? Besides, the girl looked so innocent, so helpful.

"Who are you? What is your name?" Juliana asked.

"Do you not know who I am, Mother?" The child answered, pausing to tilt her perfect head to the side. She stepped toward Juliana, her hand lifted so that it pressed warmly against Juliana's stomach when she neared. Her eyes sparkled like stars in the moonlight. "I am your daughter. Anja. And I've come to take us home."

CB80BO

Ari took a deep breath, feeling that Lucien was gone. Slowly, she shook, shrugging out of the chains he had tried to trap her with. The ache in her heart was gone the moment she had stabbed it, but within that knife's blade, she saw its fate. It was always said that when a nymph died they saw what must be done, only then it was too late to do it. Mia had died, but Lucien brought Ari back, carrying Mia's memories.

In many ways, almost all, she was Mia still. But being Mia meant having the memories of a blessed life and Ari couldn't do it anymore. She needed to cut that part of her past from her memory. She still felt, still had the partial soul, but to embrace the new name gave her hope of surviving the future in Lucien's dark world.

She touched her chest, healed from the wound. Lucien revived her body, just as she feared he would. It was as he'd always claimed. Death could not claim her, not until he let it. She was his. Forever. Eternal. His.

She slowly stood. Her gown healed itself from his claw marks and the staining blood dripped off it like water beading on metal, rolling onto the floor. Dark kohl lines drew over her flesh, twirling and winding along her right arm to decorate it in ancient vinework. The black lined her eyes and crimson replaced the smudged black Lucien had put on her lips.

Ari moved through the hanging gauze, knowing her place was not chained to the bed as a slave, but in Lucien's dark hall. She felt the palace guests, their darkness, and knew that Lucien plotted his evil plans. King Ean and his men were doomed. Queen Juliana and her baby were all but lost as the evil soothsayer led her to the Fire Palace. The Immortal Realm was crumbling all around them. Damnation was winning and her place was at its side.

Cぷꙩꙅ

Adal crept through the bowels of the palace, glancing at the crudely drawn map in his hand. He motioned to the left, indicating that Brodor should go. The elf did without hesitation, his sword gripped at his side. Adal carried a dagger clenched in his fist as he moved to follow. Screams echoed all around them and he wished he could free all those who were being tortured. There was no time for such grand heroism. They were here to save Prince Wolfe and bring him safely home.

Glancing at the map, Adal motioned to the right. The tiny hall led to a single door. Under his breath, he muttered, "This is it." Brodor reached for the latch, but Adal grabbed his wrist, shaking his head in denial. "It's a trap."

Reaching into his tunic, Adal pulled out the satchel of magic Ean had given him and opened it. He took a tiny bit of magic from its contents. Touching the soft piece of severed flesh to the door once, he put it back into the satchel, not liking the feel of dark magic on his fingers. The door creaked open and Brodor pushed it along with the tip of his sword.

"The prince," Brodor said the instant they saw Wolfe huddled along the far wall. His words sounded almost as if he hadn't really expected to find him in the dungeon. Prince Wolfe's eyes opened, dazed as he stared at the two elfin guards. He didn't move, didn't acknowledge them. Brodor thrust his sword at Adal and moved quickly forward, bowing his head slightly as he came onto one knee. "My old friend, you live."

Wolfe blinked several times, his mouth opening as if he would speak, but no sound came out with his shallow breath. He tried to lift his hand toward the warrior, but it fell back into his lap.

Brodor nodded. Reaching forward, he pulled the prince across his back to lift him up on his shoulders. Grabbing a thigh and an arm, he carried him out of the small cell. "I have him. Let us leave."

Adal didn't need to look at the map as he led the way out of the prisons. It was time to get Prince Wolfe home.

CBEOBO

Lucien's breath caught as Ari showed herself in his hall. How had she escaped the chains? Had he unconsciously freed her? And her gown? His body tight, he gripped the arms of his throne. Beneath him, the orgy had stopped and many of the demons had left his hall. Only the lycanthrope clan stayed behind, awaiting his command to attack those in the forest. With passions slaked, their normally hot tempers were calmed.

One of the beasts growled, making a move as if to go toward the woman but Andret, the clan leader, reached out and stopped him. A loud growl sounded in warning, as he gripped the man's arm and jerked violently back. Stepping forward, Andret stood before the others, his dark eyes streaked with glowing blue as he stared at Ari.

Lucien watched her approach, his chin lowered, his fingers pressed along the half smile on his lips. She moved with ease, her head high, almost regal. The gray and black gown he'd given her was repaired, only now the collar came up high in the back, framing her face. Dark curls were piled high with bangs falling forward, sweeping across to almost hide one of her kohl-lined violet eyes.

His hand fell forward as she stopped at the bottom of the steps leading to his raised throne. There was no hesitance in her as she bowed her head and curtsied. "My king."

As she stood, her eyes seemed to flash with a playful light. Lucien found himself standing. Slowly, he stepped down to meet her, aware of his demons' watchful gazes.

"Mi...?" he began softly, only to correct himself. "Ari, what are you doing in the hall?"

"I'm taking my place," she answered, without flinching, "as Mistress of the Damned King. Where else would I be but at your side, entertaining the guests of the Fire Palace?" She tilted her head thoughtfully. "Or do you wish for me to sit at your feet?"

"You want something." His tone dipped in amusement. "I know my nymph."

"We all want things, my king."

"Have you come to barter with me for King Ean and his men? You wish for me to spare them?" Lucien tossed his head back, laughing. He would not stop his plans, no matter how prettily she pleaded with him. "Even now, on the eve of your death, you come to me with thoughts of others? It would seem you are not so broken as you appeared. What price will you pay for the Blessed King's freedom?"

"None," she answered, her voice loud and clear.

A roar of laughter sounded over the hall, led by Lucien's own amusement. He stepped past her. His hand lifted as he neared the center fire pit, surging the fire so it rose higher, lighting all the gruesome faces around him in pale orange. A wolf-man howled.

Lucien turned his back to the flames. Ari hadn't moved from her place before his throne. Her arms were unmoving at her sides. "Surely, nymph, you do not think I would free the Blessed King simply because you ask it of me."

"Did I ask?" Her head turned, her eyes meeting his.

Lucien was intrigued. What was happening with his little nymph? There was something different about her, a darkness that had not been in her before. She was achingly beautiful, poised, regal, and yet he found he missed the trembling, hopeless caring of Mia.

The dark temptress before him tilted her head and laughed, mimicking his movements as she held her hands to the side, walking toward the fire. "What care I for King Ean and his men? Is my life blessed? Is my soul light?" She neared him, her face inches from his as she leaned in to whisper loudly, "Nay, methinks they are not, my king. Light has been banished by the dark. You made sure to kill it."

Lucien felt the demons' approval, heard it in the soft grunts of the lycans. A sharp pain entered him and for a moment he was blinded by it. Then he realized it was his own agony radiating though every fiber of his body. He had indeed killed a piece of his nymph, the light, the caring, the fight. Everything he'd tried to make her now stood before him—accepting her place, accepting him. But even as he still wanted her, he felt actual pain at the loss of her goodness. Part of him, by his very damned nature, liked when she betrayed him, when she defied him.

"And if I kill the Blessed King, his men and his princely brother who even now is being rescued from my dungeons?" he said, quieter than before. Lucien touched her cheek, so warm to his cold.

"So be it. Fate has called for their deaths and their deaths it will have." Ari lowered her lashes, sweeping them seductively over her violet eyes. "But, you are right, there is one thing, one small, little thing I do wish to have."

Anything, he thought.

"What?" he asked.

"If you give it to me to do with as I wish, I will stay here in your hall by your side, at your feet, wherever you shall put me. No more escaping. No more betrayal."

"And if I take a Bellemare soul?"

At that she hesitated. "Then they were foolish for losing their soul to you. I will not stop you, even if it is in my power."

"You will choose me?" He didn't dare let any of the others hear the question as he leaned close to her ear.

"Aye," she said just as softly. "You."

"Why?"

"It is my place. My choices led me here. I bartered my soul. I gave it to you. Methought you would kill me, but you kept me alive. So, here I am, as is your will, and here I will remain until you see fit to kill me."

"Do you," he hesitated, "think to love...?"

"There is no love in this world, Lucien, you know as well as I do. We dark beings are not capable of it."

Lucien knew that was not true. Love was not only an emotion of the blessed. For certain, such creatures of light held a purer love than evil ever could. But, the dark could love. Vanity could be love. Obsession could be love. Desire could be love. Even as he thought it, he did not correct her.

"You have my word," she said. "I will be loyal."

"What is it you wish from me?" Lucien knew he would give her whatever she asked for. He always gave in to her, in the end.

"I want the instrument of my death." Her eyes lit, catching the firelight from the center pit behind him. "I want the jeweled dagger. Queen Juliana's dagger."

"Why?" He didn't move. "What need have you for it?"

"To do with as I wish. The blade stilled my beating heart and I saw all that the knife is meant to do. There is death in its steel and I want it." She pouted her lip, her gaze eager. "Give it to me, Lucien, as a present. I want it."

Lucien thought for a moment before lifting his hand to the side. Flames wrapped his fingers before forming into the blade. The rough texture of the jewels rubbed against his palm. Her eyes moved to it, but he didn't give it to her. Instead, he walked back toward the throne. Ari followed behind, slow and not as sure. He heard it in her breathing, in the way her feet stepped quietly on the stone floor.

"I would like to present Lady Ari," Lucien announced, swinging around to face the hall. "Mistress of the Fire Palace."

The demons cheered, the lycans howled, Ari's eyes met his. Pointing the dagger's tip at the floor, he willed a chair to grow from the black stone, its carved back matching the demon and flame pattern of his own seat. The platform widened, the steps moving over to make room. With his free hand, he motioned her to join him, at his side, in a seat of honor that no other had ever taken.

"Mistress," Lucien said, as she paused one step beneath the platform. He held the dagger to her, staring at her mouth as she smiled. Her fingers wrapped around the presented hilt, the long nails brushing the back of his hand as he let go.

"My king." Ari eyed the blade.

Lucien sat, glancing next to him to indicate that she should do the same. Ari ignored the chair, instead sitting on his lap for all to see. He tensed, continually surprised by her change. His thighs parted, letting her butt fit next to his stiff erection. She giggled softly to feel it, clutching her new knife in her fist. Lifting it to his throat, she kept her gaze steady on his. Steel grazed his flesh, but did not cut. She awaited his permission to cut. Closing his eyes as a rush of potent desire overcame him, he tilted his neck to the side. She could not kill him with the blade, but if she were to slice open his throat, she would weaken him, allowing for King Ean and his men's possible escape.

She chuckled and he knew she understood his vulnerability. The blade cut, drawing a line over his neck, scratching the surface enough to make it bleed, but not enough to drain his energies. Wrapping her hand along his cheek, she leaned to his throat and licked. Fire sparked in Lucien's gaze at the intense pleasure of her acceptance. Her lush mouth sucked gently, drinking him.

The beast within surged forth, evident in his voice as he ordered, "Andret, they have made it outside the palace walls and are tired. I call the moon over Hades so that you may have its strength for your shift. You have your orders, see that you do not fail me."

"My king." Andret bowed, before turning to his clan. Throwing back his head, he howled loud and long. The lycanthrope voices joined their leader's as they hurried from the hall so that they may greet the moonlight and shift into their full terrifying forms.

"The rest of you, leave us!" he ordered.

Ari pulled back, her mouth stained with his blood, the knife gripped in her delicate hand. "Show me what happened in the hall today. I smell the sex. I see the altars. Show me."

Lucien drew flames from the center pits to the altars, allowing them to form into creatures of the past. The flames moved like a life-size fire play, letting her see and hear the claiming of the dark faeries as they became impregnated with the first of his half-breed army. Lucien did not make the fire dance, merely watched the cruel actions of others with it. Lucien's face became marred with the beast inside him.

"You have never asked to see these things before." He angled his mouth for her bloody kiss. It was true, she'd often begged him to stop watching the cruel acts of others within the flames.

"As a nymph, it is a sin for me to find pleasure in the arms of a Damned King," she said, instead of answering his observation. "Come, Lucien, help me to sin again."

CRIEN

"The lycans attack!" Levin ran toward King Ean. Even as the shout sounded clouds drifted over the sky, carrying with it the evening moon. "Hurry, my king, we must get you away."

Tensing, Ean sniffed the air, catching the faintest scent of wolf on the breeze. But that wasn't all, he caught the smell of his elfin guard. "Grab the unicorns!"

Levin was already halfway toward the animals, signaling them to follow him toward the king. "We must ride."

"I feel Adal approaching." Ean swung onto the unicorn's bare back, knowing the riderless two would follow his mount wherever he galloped. Kicking the steed in the side, he held onto the horn as the animal took off, passing over Hades' borders toward the Fire Palace.

"My king!" Levin yelled. "They will meet us back at the encampment. We must keep you safe."

"They have my brother!" Ean pressed down, urging the unicorn faster. Hooves beat heavily over the solid earth, as the dead grasses of the brown prairie sped by. Desperate he rode, following his feelings to find Wolfe and his guards. Silver moonlight shone overhead, the moon full and bright. Such a swift moonrise could only have been borne of magic and there was no guessing whose magic it was. Lucien knew they took Wolfe and he sent the lycans to stop them.

Seeing three shadowed figures running, one being pulled by a larger, he slowed his hurried pace. Wolves howled, barking into the night. He heard their feet, but couldn't see them.

"Adal!" Ean shouted. The commander jumped as his unicorn hurried toward him, landing gracefully on the animal's back. Levin was behind him, approaching but still far off. Motioning the other unicorn forward, he hollered, "Brodor!"

138

As the unicorn ran for the old warrior, Wolfe tripped, falling to the side. Brodor, who had a hold of the prince's hand, was jerked back by the motion. The dark brown of his clothing made it impossible to make him out on the ground. Their figures disappeared into the prairie grasses. Ean continued forward, nudging his mount to once more pick up speed.

Suddenly, a loud growl sounded as three large wolves leapt in the moonlight. The unicorns spooked, the one heading for Brodor reared on its hind legs. A loud scream sounded. Brodor appeared, his fist striking out.

"Get up, Wolfe!" Brodor fought the animal with his bare hands before gaining enough room to free his sword.

Ean reached behind his back, grabbing his sword. An arrow shot past him as Levin caught up to the skirmish. A lycan yelped in surprise, flipping back over tail.

Jumping off the unicorn, while holding its horn in one hand and his weapon in the other, Ean kicked his feet, making contact with the lycan injured by the arrow. He landed near his brother. Wolfe moaned, his wide eyes staring up at the night sky. Ean reached to lift him up, only to hesitate briefly as his hands met with blood. Wolfe was wounded. "Wolfe, come."

Brodor fought near them, slashing his sword wide to keep a particularly bloodthirsty lycan back. The creature's eyes glowed blue, burning with hunger. "More approach. Protect the king—*ah!*"

The beast lurched forward, sinking his teeth into the elf's shoulder. Brodor shouted an ancient battle cry asking for strength, before plunging his sword into his attacker's hairy side.

"I have him." Levin shot arrows past Ean.

"Brodor!" Adal galloped near with his hand out. The old warrior shrugged the wolf's body off him, reaching his wounded arm up so that he wasn't forced to drop his sword. He swung up behind the commander with a grunt.

Ean managed to get Wolfe onto the mount, while the lycan was distracted with Brodor, before seating himself behind him. He hugged his brother to his chest and it took all his efforts to keep them both seated as he urged the unicorn to gallop toward the Mystic forest and away from Kingdom of Hades' borderlands.

Desperately whispering as they rode, Ean said, "Hold, Wolfe, hold. I have you. It is over. I will not let anything more happen to you. I promise."

CRSOBO

"Why do you laugh?" Ari asked, leaning back from where she straddled Lucien's thighs on his throne. The hall was empty and they were both naked. Small cuts littered their bodies, injuries from when they made love. She gripped the jeweled dagger tight. "King Ean and his men escaped. The lycanthropes failed."

"Nay," Lucien said. "They did not fail. They did exactly what I asked of them."

"But, King Ean is alive. That is what you wanted?" She eyed his face, aroused by the look of crimson on his lips.

"If the king dies, the unblessed will win the war and it will end. That does not suit my designs, sweet mistress." He touched her cheek. "All is as I plan."

Ari lifted the knife, chuckling. "I always wanted to try this." Smoke swirled from her hand, creating a tiny flame. The trick was nothing compared to his great power, as she sent the dagger away. Pouting slightly, she lowered her lids. "I want more power, Lucien. Give me more power."

He grinned. "All in time, nymph, all in time."

Chapter Nine

"What is this place?" Juliana asked Anja, eyeing the weeping trees of the forest leading to a stone prairie. The tall grasses were like sharp blades shooting up from the ground, yet so delicate she could kick them over, breaking them with her toes. "It does not feel right. I do not think we should go here."

"This is the dead lands. They are meant to scare you away, to keep you from finding the way out of this place." Anja motioned her to follow. The child didn't say much, but did smile whenever she saw Juliana looking in her direction, which was often. "See, there, in the distance? The castle?"

"Aye."

"It is a palace. In its great hall there is a stone fire. That is the way back to the Realm of Immortals. That will take you home." Anja smiled, her blue eyes shining.

Juliana nodded. She followed the child's lead as the girl led her into the prairie, kicking over the stone grasses with each sweeping step.

C3ΩΩ80

"Thomas, what has happened? Why have you come to Feia?" Hugh stood, rushing around the dining table to greet his brother. He looked worn, his eyes red.

"William." Thomas' expression was strained. "You sent a missive, asking him why he had yet to come. He left sennights ago. If he is not here, then—"

"William arrived," Hugh said to put his brother at ease. "Late, but did arrive."

"Oh, thank the heavens," Thomas sighed in obvious relief. Then, his brow wrinkling in surprise, he pointed at Hugh. "You have wings."

"One word about them and I'll—" Hugh began.

"Tania says Thomas is—" William stopped as he came around the corner from the stairwell, his clothes sloppily hanging on his frame. "Ho, Thomas, what brings you to Feia?"

"You," Thomas said.

"Me?" William glanced around, as if his brother couldn't possibly mean him.

"Aye, Hugh sent a missive saying you never arrived. You left sennights ago."

"What took you so long?" Hugh asked.

Tania flew past William's head, smiling as she veered off her course toward Hugh to go to Thomas. "Thomas, my brother, welcome. It has been too long."

Thomas managed a small smile for the faery queen. "Tania, as lovely as ever."

"William," Hugh said, turning everyone's attention back to the subject. "What took you?"

"It's nothing. Just something I had to take care of."

"In this realm? What?" Thomas asked, striding across the hall toward William. "Did you find a way to free Juliana?"

"Nay, it had nothing to do with Juliana." William glanced away, biting his lip.

"By all that is holy, Will, tell us what you were doing," Hugh demanded. His wings fluttered. Thomas put his hand over his mouth to keep from chuckling as he stared at Hugh's back.

"It is a personal matter." William tried to refuse.

"William!" Hugh yelled.

"Lord Angus discovered I have been coming to Feia to visit you. His men have been watching the palace and when I came, they took me." William shrugged. "It is naught to be concerned over."

"My faeries have seen no one in the forest." Tania landed by her husband.

"They're giants." William crossed his arms over his chest. "They're huge. They can see far. I know, I was a giant once." He waved his hand, frowning. "Or four times. I lose count. There was a lot of drinking that fortnight."

"Angus? The giant whose daughter you—?" Hugh began.

"I swear the baby is not mine," William interrupted. "But do you think he'll listen? He insists I marry the woman. So, when they discovered I was coming here in secret, they stole me away to Lord Angus so that I might face these imaginary crimes."

"You were held up by an angry father?" Thomas asked, trying not to smirk.

"A giant angry father," William defended. "I swear on Bellemare that is all that happened. I was detained by Lord Angus and then I came straight here."

"How did you escape?" Tania asked.

"I, ah…" William shrugged. "It matters not."

"How?" Hugh tried not to laugh.

"I agreed to marry the woman as soon as I finish my wizard apprenticeship." William lifted his hand, hurrying to add, "But the true jest is mine. I'm mortal. I will not live long enough to finish my apprenticeship."

Hugh's features fell some at the mention of mortality. Unless fate intervened and he was murdered, he would live forever, unchanging. The trade-off was seeing his brothers age and die like men die. Covering the emotions, he grinned, holding his arms to the sides. "Both my brothers here in my home. Come, this calls for a feast."

"We'll drink to Juliana," Tania said.

The men's expressions fell at her words. Hugh knew she meant no harm by them. Tania grew up in this realm, where magical spells happened, people became lost and later were found. But this was Juliana, their sister. Sweet Juliana. Precious, perfect Juliana. A celebration did not feel right without her.

"Mayhap just a drink," Thomas answered.

"Aye," William agreed. "A drink."

"To our sister," Hugh said. "To our Juliana."

CR∞BO

"I should tell you exactly how I escaped the prisons," Ari said.

Lucien felt her moving around their bedchamber, but did not take his eyes from the fireplace. He already knew, and yet he still said, "I have wondered."

"William the Wizard found a way into the dungeons," she said.

Lucien glanced in her direction, lazily winding trails of fire between his fingers. He lounged in his chair, the firelight warming his chilled flesh. Wearing only his unlaced breeches for comfort, he shifted his weight, crossing an ankle over his knee.

All was going according to his plan. The half-breed army was begun, the two faery mothers hidden safe within the mortal world, worshiped in demon temples. Even the border between the Immortal Realm and Bellemare was beginning to blur. The more protection spells Sir Thomas cast, the more magic that was used, the more the boundary between the worlds slipped. Soon their protection magic would be undone by itself and his demons would be able to cross over, carrying with them fire and darkness. Bellemare would be lost, the mortal world a living hell.

"He took me out through the fireplace when it surged," she continued when he didn't answer.

"Did he?"

"Aye. He felt he owed me for saving him. He wanted me to go with him. I wanted to, I considered it, but I sent him away." Ari moved, dancing between the columns of gauze, disappearing and reappearing within his vision. There was a carefree feeling to her graceful movements as her bare feet swept over the rough stone. Unconsciously, he willed the floor to smooth for her. She smiled, flashing her violet eyes in his direction.

"Because you knew I'd find you?"

"You have my soul." Ari turned, coming back through the gauze. "There is no escape for me."

"Hm." He didn't smile, instead piercing her with his gaze as he detected every change in her movement and expression.

"You would have left me there, wouldn't you? I'd be there still if William had not come." She stopped her pretty movements to look at him, waiting for an answer.

Lucien closed his eyes, only to open them as he looked at the fire. She would never know the truth, never know that it was he disguised as William who freed her. No one would ever know. "Aye. I would have left you down there. Mayhap forever."

C3⤳80

Mystic Forest

"They are getting worse, aren't they?" Ean looked at his brother's pale face shaded by the thin canvas tent hanging down from the thick branches overhead. The grass beneath them was as soft a bed as the Blessed King could find. The sounds of the forest, of insects humming, of a far off bird, of leaves crashing, carried forth on the warm breeze as it drifted over through the thick of the trees.

According to Adal, he'd looked near dead from his time in the Fire Palace and now, combined with the infected claw and bite marks on his body, he appeared almost corpse-like. Only the shallow rise and fall of his chest showed he lived.

Next to Wolfe was Brodor. He had suffered fewer wounds, and had been in fine shape to begin with, but still his pallor was bad. He didn't move, lying just as still as the rescued prince.

"No matter what we try, the wounds do not heal. We can manage to stop the bleeding, but only for short periods." Adal wiped his bloodied hands on a piece of torn tunic. "I've sent Levin back to the forest for more herbs."

"We need a healer." Ean frowned, looking at his own bloodstained hands.

Michelle M. Pillow

"At the encampment—"

"Nay," Ean stopped the commander from finishing. He watched, but Wolfe did not move. "We need healers who understand this kind of infection. We are using all the herbs they would use back at our encampment. None of it helps."

Ean left the makeshift tent. The forest was dense—too dense to see through. He strode toward a clear, still stream that curled from the trees only to cut a path back into them. Along the shores were wide paths. The dirt floor was covered with the littering of leaves and twigs. Sunlight shone in from the break in the trees, glistening like liquid crystals on the top of the glassy water. A log had fallen over the stream at a shallow point to make a natural bridge between the two shores. Ean's foot slipped in the moss that grew along the water's stony edge, but he caught himself before he fell.

"You wish to seek out a dark healer?" Adal said. He'd followed him out of the tent, joining him along the stream. Kneeling on a flat rock, he put his bloodied hands in the water, rinsing them. "But, who can we trust? It's clear the wizard told Lucien of our coming, or in the very least allowed us to be seen by the Damned King. Those lycans were waiting for us outside the palace. They knew we'd be there."

"I do not think we have a choice." Ean watched the pink water drift past, carrying the blood away. He crouched, keeping both feet on the ground as he leaned against his knees. He put both hands in the water, wiggling his fingers. "We must go to Merrick."

"What? But we are at war," Adal protested. He dried his hands on his stained tunic, doing his best to avoid the bloody spots. "You would go to the unblessed for—"

"Wolfe is his brother as much as mine. I know you do not believe me, but I have felt good in Merrick. He may hate me, but

148

he will not turn Wolfe away. I can only hope to learn what magic he knows to heal Brodor as well." Ean sighed, the decision sitting heavily upon his conscience. "Send Levin back to the encampment with the news that we live and will be joining them shortly. We will tell no one of this trip to Valdis."

"And if King Merrick does not agree to help us?"

"He might not help us, but he will help Wolfe." Ean stood, flicking the water from his hands. "Even if I was certain he'd throw me in his dungeons, I would still go. I would forfeit my life for Wolfe's or Ladon's." It wasn't a lie. Now that Ean had found his brothers, both after so long, he could not lose them. "Let us ready some cots for Wolfe and Brodor. We will ride slow and steady toward Valdis and hope Merrick detects us before we get there."

CЗՑᏴ

The ache inside Merrick grew, even as the scratches he tried so desperately to keep embedded into his chest began to fade. He'd called Lord Kalen back to help him, needing his trusted friend at his side. It wasn't as if he could contact Lucien and ask nicely for Juliana's dagger. He was going to need magic and lots of it.

Singing filled his hall, the sweet sounds of a mermaid and her two nymph companions. The mermaid, a dark skinned favorite of Lord Kalen, sat on the stone ground with her purple and silver tail swishing in the pool of water he'd created for her in the main hall's floor. Two others sat beside her. A redhead with her legs drawn up, barely covered by the clinging white material of her gown, and a petite blonde with incredible lips, who dipped one naked foot into the water while resting her chin on her knee.

They were the same three who sang the night he held a banquet for Juliana, and the tinkling of their joined voices rang torture over him as he remembered that night. The language was an ancient water language that cast a small spell that invoked those who listened into dancing.

It was before Juliana accepted her place by his side as queen, when he'd introduced her to his subjects. Closing his eyes, hearing the music, he pictured her as she'd been.

Curls had been piled high on top of her head, cascading down the back in long ringlets threaded with blue ribbons. The heavy sapphire necklace and matching ring she had worn were still in the palace vault. The jewels matched the dark blue gown Merrick had materialized for her. Starting just off her shoulder, the sheer material had fallen gracefully down past her wrist to hide her hand. The same fabric overlaid the skirt and fluttered over the darker satin as she danced. A slight smile crossed his face as he remembered the bodice. He'd made it low, the square cut showcasing her breasts, but she'd begged him to lift the material higher against her throat, as if hiding the suggestive cleavage would diminish his desire for her.

He had made the gown dark blue to match her eyes and it had, bringing out the color. Her gaze had sparkled like the stars he called down from the heavens for her. He had rearranged the heavens and earth for her, much to the anger of the wizards, and he would do it again if he had to.

Thinking of her like that, he unconsciously changed his clothes to what they had been that night. His tight breeches and shirt remained black, but he wore a long sleeveless overtunic that hung open in the front, falling to the ground like a cape. The dark material was embroidered with dark blue, the front held together by two silver chains that draped over his chest. An up-turned collar framed his face and leather bound back the sides of his long hair, winding down the length from his temples to just above his waist. Cool metal wrapped his forehead, crossing from temple to temple with a dark blue sapphire appearing in the center.

"Interesting choice in decoration, my king."

Merrick blinked in slight confusion at the sound of Lord Kalen's voice. But his friend did not speak of the king's new attire, as his gaze was on the old crone hung upside down before the singing women. Thick chains held her to the ceiling, allowing her to swing back and forth. She'd given up trying to escape the hour before and now just hung, silent and grimacing.

"Though, would you mind covering up her back end. It does not make for a very welcoming sight." Kalen motioned his thumb at the crone but, as his eyes moved to the singing women, his expression changed. He grinned at the dark mermaid. She smiled back at him, batting her purple-tinted lashes. When he looked back at the king, he arched a playful brow as he mouthed his thanks.

"I'm only getting started with her." Merrick had placed the hem of the crone's gown into the ankle chains but it must have slipped out of the back. He motioned his hand, covering the problem. The witch struggled at his words, the chains rattling anew as she glared at him. He knew she wanted to speak, but her mouth was bound shut with a ring of stone. "When I'm finished, she'll be broken."

"Tell me how I should cross you, my king, so that I would deserve such a punishment." Kalen again looked at the mermaid, biting his lip.

"I did not summon you here for pleasantries," Merrick said.

"I know." Kalen's expression fell some. He lifted his hand, fingers up.

"I will order her to your bed for a century if you help me…" Merrick hesitated.

"Tell me," Kalen said.

Merrick lifted his hand and waited as the thin thread of light wrapped over them, telling Kalen all he needed to know. The nobleman instantly turned to where the witch hung upside down. The light disappeared and Kalen slowly pulled his shaking hand away, not bothering to look back at the king.

"What you are asking of me…" Kalen whispered.

"Aye, I know." Merrick was sorry for it, but he needed to know the truth. He needed Juliana's dagger. Lifting his hand, he materialized a drink for his friend. Kalen glanced at it, but did not touch it. "I cannot do it, Kalen. I have not the gift. But I will give you anything you ask for."

"Send them away. Stop their singing." Kalen took a deep breath, striding over the stone. The carefree giant had been replaced by the efficient movements of a soldier with purpose.

"Ladies," Merrick ordered. Their voices stopped mid-note as they looked at him. They nodded in unison. The king waved his hand and the three singers disappeared, taking their stone pond with them, as he returned them home.

"Remove the stone. Let her speak." Kalen stood before the witch, reaching to pull the blindfold from her missing eyes as Merrick removed her stone gag. The elf dropped the ragged cloth on the floor. The witch sniffed him, grinning a mouthful of rotted teeth.

"Bind her hands," Kalen said. Merrick did, beckoning black chains from the floor to wrap her wrists, jerking them hard to the side.

"Aye, psychic, read of me," the crone taunted. "I have marvelous things to show you. An eternity of my deeds before you find the one you want. I will taint you. I will be in your dreams."

"Anything I want?" Kalen said to Merrick, giving a weak laugh as he glanced back. "Can you take the gift away? Can you stop the images I see?"

Merrick stood. "If I could grant such a thing, I would, but I cannot—"

The words were interrupted as Kalen laid his hands on the witch, gripping her wrinkled cheeks. The nobleman's body stiffened. The flames in the five fireplaces stopped moving, their light over the hall unchanging as Kalen began to chant. Merrick slowly walked around, watching as the dark elf read the woman. The droning sound of the nobleman's voice was drowned out by the sounds of the witch's laughter as she tried to jerk away.

Suddenly, the crone screamed, as if her soulless heart were being ripped from her chest. Her arms shook, blood trickling down the black chains as the metal cut into her wrists, dripping with increasing rapidity onto the floor. Kalen's fingers dug into her flesh, drawing more blood with his nails. The dark, long length of his hair shook with each of his movements. Red began at his roots, spreading down from the crown over the brown length, the crimson color flowing over his wavy locks like blood.

The witch's eye sockets bled, dripping down her forehead. Kalen let out a loud cry as the witch did the same. The blood tears rolled over his cheeks, cutting alongside his mouth. He gasped, pulling away from the horrible woman as he stumbled back.

The king made a move to go to him, wishing he could have done it himself. He sensed the deep agony the nobleman felt. Kalen lifted his hand to stop Merrick's advance, as he fell to the ground. "Do not. No more. I cannot be touched. I do not want to see any more."

Kalen wiped his nose on his sleeve. Merrick motioned forward, materializing a cloth before his arm was completely extended. He dropped it on the floor near the man. Fighting the need to ask him to hurry and reveal what he'd learned, the king forced himself to hold back.

"She's locked the queen in a world of stone," Kalen said.

"We know this much. She's—"

"Nay, the queen is awake in a stone world. She sees us as statues, but she's here in the palace." Kalen pressed his palms against his head, groaning slightly. "Nay, she *was* here in the palace until recently. Dark spirits were sent to frighten her away. Only two others can enter the stone world." He pointed weakly at the witch. "The crone and her counterpart, a childlike creature that lives in the Fire Palace."

"Too late, too late," the witch cackled.

"To know the future is to know madness," Kalen whispered, his words rambling and slurred as he talked more to himself than Merrick, "for there are things that cannot be changed. But, to see the past and present, to feel the darkness that will not be altered, to know there is no hope of fighting the deeds that are already done. Sometimes it is better not to reveal."

"Kalen, please, I must know," Merrick insisted.

"You, in your pain, made a glorious infusion to the witch's power." Kalen breathed heavily. "She fed off your misery and would be feeding still. I feel how you love and want your wife. Only, the witch didn't count on your love for Juliana being so strong. Since you faced the crone in her den, your feelings have weakened her. Her guard was down and I felt, I saw... They have yet to finish..."

"What?" Merrick demanded.

"It is not done," Kalen said.

"What is not done?" The king stood above him.

"The evil child leads the queen toward King Lucien where he waits for her." The nobleman looked up, his dark eyes bloodshot and encircled with black. Blood marred his flesh. "If the girl gets Queen Juliana to jump into the fire in the palace's main hall, Lucien can draw her out. The baby is overdue and will kill her almost instantly, but Lucien will have power over the child to keep or dispose of as he pleases."

"Tell him," the crone demanded. "Tell him all, psychic."

"What else did you see?" Merrick demanded. "Tell me."

"Lucien will kill the child." Kalen looked away. "A sacrifice to the blackest magic to help him create a demon army of half breeds. I saw your son, my king." A tear slipped down Kalen's cheek, pinked with blood. "I saw blood on him. But I cannot be certain. It was a fragment. Hands and blood."

Merrick's ears rang. Kill Juliana? Kill his son? His body weak, he didn't even have the strength to unlock his knees and fall to the ground. He thought of the vision he saw when first he learned of the possibility of Juliana's pregnancy. He'd asked to see the future, to see his son, in hopes of gleaning when it might be. All he got was the image of Juliana screaming, tears falling over her pale cheeks. Then he saw his own hands covered in blood. And now Lucien's words confirmed his worst fears.

Merrick felt the world spinning past him, felt the magic, his rule, the forces of fate and destiny. Suddenly, the realm felt too big. Helplessness did not suit him, but he could not fight its effects as they seized upon his heart.

"Merrick, you must find your brother and bring him here. The only way we can free her is with King Ean's blood."

"But, Juliana's knife…" Merrick was spurred into action. A blade formed along his side, growing with a scabbard at his waist as he readied himself to ride out.

"Check behind your throne," Kalen said.

Merrick waved his hand, striding across the floor. His throne disappeared, revealing a knife behind it. "How?"

"I do not know," Kalen admitted. "I merely felt it there when I searched the crone's power for its location."

"What?" the witch screamed. "Nay, you cannot!"

"Quiet, hag," Merrick ordered, slapping another stone gag over her throat, letting it squeeze tight in his anger. She struggled anew, but could not escape. The Unblessed King pressed his wife's dagger against his chest, letting the material of his tunic swallow it against his flesh. A scabbard formed, protecting his chest from the blade while holding it into place. "Are you well enough to ride?"

Kalen pushed to his feet swaying back and forth. "Do not ask it of me. I will be of little use astride a horse."

"Then stay. Mend." Merrick began to reach for Kalen, only to stop before touching him. He tried to help him, but there was little the Unblessed King could do. Shouting, he ordered, "Iago! Come!"

"Aye." The old goblin wobbled around the corner into the hall. It was no surprise to the king that his unblessed subjects had been spying on the torturous show. For once, he didn't care what they overheard. There were more important matters than goblin gossip. More of the small creatures ambled in behind Iago, coming though they were not summonsed.

"Anything Lord Kalen wants, fetch for him. He has free run of this castle." Merrick walked past them toward the front gate. "Kalen, I'll take your horse."

"Back away," Kalen ordered. Merrick glanced back in time to see Iago rolling away from the elf noble. Undoubtedly, the goblin had touched him.

The others began to dance around the witch, their small arms and legs pumping excitedly as they shouted taunts. Each tried to outdo the other, seeing who could insult her the worst.

"Fate," Merrick whispered so none could hear him. He strode down the narrow passageway, intent on going to the battlefront to find his brother. "Since taking my reign, I have never asked for anything from you. But today I am begging. Help me find Ean and free my family. Do not let Lucien harm Juliana and our son. Even if it is your desire that I do not have her for myself, do not let death take her." He ran faster. "Please, fate, keep her safe."

Chapter Ten

"Prince Wolfe is getting worse," Adal reported, coming from the makeshift cot strapped to the back of King Ean's unicorn. His nose was red and his eyes watered from the nip of the cold wind. "I can barely feel his heart beating."

Brodor was behind Adal's mount, strapped to a cot like Wolfe. Both ill men were covered from neck to foot, their wounds bandaged and hidden from view. Adal had constructed a canopy over their faces, blocking them from the weather.

The landscape had become dismal, matching their dark moods, as rain pelted the ground. Gray, sinister skies consumed the day hours, turning the ground into a seemingly bottomless pit of sticky black mud. The muck blemished the glistening coats of the unicorns and clung to the riders' tunics. Thick trails dug into the path where the end of the cots pressed into the earth with the weight of their cargo.

"The Black Palace is close. I can feel its unblessing." Ean took a deep breath, even as his entire being seemed to sicken the closer they went toward Merrick's palace. Cold soaked his clothing and he cursed the wizards for choosing today to make foul weather. The land needed rain as much as it needed light, but why today? The cold air pressed against his face, stinging his cheeks to a sharp red. He worried that his brother and friend might catch their death in the evening wind. They were too weak from the lycan's bites and the Blessed King smelled mortality on their still forms. "Even the trees seem sick with despair and sadness. It is as if the heavens cry."

"And King Merrick? Do you sense him?" Adal asked. "Is he near?"

"I..." Ean frowned. "I am not sure. All of this feels of Merrick—every leaf, every stone, every droplet of rain—but I cannot say where he is. We must go toward the Black Palace. Merrick will feel me and he will come. How can he not?"

Even as he said the words, he wasn't so sure. It was possible his brother would ignore him.

"Or if he will not come to me, he will come if he senses Wolfe," Ean added. "How could he resist? At the very least, curiosity will bring him to us."

"He will come," Adal assured the king, though he didn't sound confident.

"Aye, he will," Ean agreed, still trying to convince himself. He looked back at Wolfe's pale, sweaty face. The prince's cheekbones were sunken, his eyes more so. *I just hope he comes in time.*

⚜

"This place..." Juliana hesitated, looking at the strange carved stone. It looked like a large fire blazing as high as the castle. With each movement of her body, she bumped against frozen droplets of stone rain. They were suspended in the air, only falling to the ground when touched. The storm had just appeared within a blink. She ran her hand in front of her, clearing a space, turning around in a circle. The stones tinkled.

When she again faced the castle, the droplets she'd cleared were replaced by others.

"This palace is meant to frighten you," Anja said, her big eyes blinking innocently. "Please, come with me." When Juliana didn't readily move, the child stepped closer and slid her hand over the queen's and tugged gently. "Please, come with me, lady mother." Anja placed a little hand on the swell of Juliana's stomach. "If you do not get out, I cannot leave. Don't you want me in your world? Don't you want me?"

Juliana took a deep breath. Every instinct told her to run, but looking down at the small hand pressed against her, so tiny and helpless, she couldn't do it. She couldn't leave the girl to fend for herself.

"Lead the way," Juliana said softly, patting the girl's soft hair. "I am right behind you."

೮೩೫೦೮೦

The atrocities he had witnessed when he touched the witch were dreams Lord Kalen would not wish upon any man or creature. Where a soul should reside was only darkness and, where a heart should be found beating, there was only pleasure derived in the suffering of others. The crone carried so much evil and now it was his. Once seen, such things could not be rid of.

Unable to stomach riding, it had been all he could do to make his way abovestairs to a guest chamber he often used when staying at the palace, not that he stayed often. The chamber was simple, with bare furnishings and a fur rug against the stone floor. At the end of the bed, a trunk stood, filled with clothes for his use. Other than a chair by the narrow slit of a window looking out from the high tower spire, there was nothing else. Kalen rested on the large bed. He ran his arm over the empty side, wishing he had company to take his thoughts from his troubles and knowing that no amount of female company could make him forget.

He thought of the mermaid, but the image wouldn't stay with him long before being replaced by demons. Kalen liked mermaids. Inside they felt as cold as the sea and open and vast as the waters that kept them. They held no thoughts for him to read, no emotions for him to feel. They were easy companions for a man like him, even if they didn't have the heart to really care past their own vanity.

Only the fire's soft crackle invaded the echoing screams in his head. The sounds weren't his, but the witch's, a small piece of what she heard when she dreamed. Kalen gave a nervous laugh, unable to do aught else. His mother called what he'd been born with a gift. He knew it to be a curse. Seeing the future held no pleasure for him. Sensing despair brought only pain. He tried to fight it, to deny his gift, but to do so made it worse. Until the insane visions invaded his life, coming to him like ghosts demanding to be heard until he couldn't detect what was real and what was only a vision.

Perhaps he really was the madman people accused him of being.

No one ever asked to know the happiness and the visions rarely saw fit to share such moments with him. But, out of all he'd seen, he had never truly looked into the abyss of evil. Tonight he had. When he touched the witch, he'd seen hell.

Pushing off the bed, he moved toward the fireplace, trying to heat his chilled skin. Nothing could erase the cold in his heart. The images crashed in on him, senseless in their timeline. Past mingled with present, future invaded the past until it was a jumbled, useless mess.

Kalen had known it would be that way, so he had focused his thoughts on Queen Juliana. The whole picture was unclear, but he'd seen pieces of what would happen. He saw her son, her baby covered in afterbirth and held by bloody hands, taken from an unmoving black form. Juliana dead? The child ripped from her stomach?

Then he saw another picture, surely before the first in time. Tears ran down her cheeks, spilling from her frightened blue eyes. She called for help, pounded her fist against the stone, screaming, pleading, begging. There was no answer to her cries, only the continual, endless screaming. No one could hear her. No one ever came.

Kalen paced the floor, his feet falling on the thick pelt. The fur was hot from the flames and he welcomed the sting of it. Closing his eyes, he let the golden heat come over him and tried to calm his anxious thoughts.

He wanted to join his king, but knew he'd be useless. Even now his limbs threatened to shake. And, with the thoughts filling his head, if he were to go near other living creatures, the thin thread left of his sanity would snap. Nay, the best way he could help his friends was to stay away from them.

On the other side of the door he detected the tiptoeing feet of a goblin. He turned his head, watching the curved handle. The creature stopped and Kalen imagined the goblin to be pressing his ear to the thick oak wood of the door. The door was locked and he would not let anyone in. Not tonight.

"Get away!" The words were hoarse. Kalen did not want to feel inside the being. "Leave me be or feel the tip of my sword for a fortnight!"

Footfalls ran quickly away, thumping down the stairwell only to disappear. He slowly crossed, unlatching the door so he could pull it open. The dark stone passageway was empty.

"Do not come up here again!" he yelled anyway, letting his voice carry. Loud irritation was a small comfort, but he took it.

As he was pulling back inside, he paused. The goblin had left a polished silver tray with a large pitcher of ale and a silver goblet etched with dragons. Kalen again looked down the passageway toward the stairwell.

"Bring more ale!" He leaned over, lifting the tray. "And I'd thank you to hurry!"

He carried the tray in, kicking the door shut behind him as he set it on the trunk. Filling the goblet, he moved to put the pitcher down. He stopped, catching his reflection looking up at him from the polished silver. Red locks wove within the brown, concentrated heavily around the crown of his head. Even his eyes were changed, the color drained until they were purple no more, but a gray.

"There is no going back," Kalen told his strange reflection, giving a weak, nearly hysterical laugh. "The witch has tainted your blood, Kalen. There is no erasing the things you have seen."

Instead of the pitcher, he set down the goblet. Lifting the larger vessel to his lips, he took a long drink of the ale, letting it warm his stomach even as he wished for something stronger. It would take more than a barrel of the stout drink to numb his brain.

CRENED

"Merrick is not going to let you in to the Black Garden to see her." Hugh sat astride his stallion. His horse was of the old Bellemare bloodline, come with him from the Mortal Realm. William had conjured some sort of air beast, invisible to their eye but who carried the wizard like a horse would. Thomas rode

163

his own horse, a younger animal with a fine, but stubborn temperament.

"We are all together," Thomas said. Though the ground was muddy and the sky wet, they were dry. Faery magic shielded them with a protective dome, causing the rain to roll around them as they rode through the forest. The surrounding forests blurred into a series of colors with each traveling droplet. "If we can somehow bring her back by all four of us siblings being together..."

"Aye," William nodded. His brown robes were pulled over his arms so that he was forced to grip his invisible reins from beneath the thick material. His long, unkempt hair flopped around his head with each bounce. "Juliana loves family. She would not want us estranged."

"I have wizards and faery elders working on how we might free her." Hugh felt guilty but not knowing why. He couldn't meet his brothers' eyes. "It is not as if I've done nothing. I've done things, dealt with creatures who..."

Hugh frowned. Though nothing too unsavory to his honor, he'd gone to questionable means for just a chance at freeing her.

"No one is condemning you, Hugh." Thomas sighed, rubbing the back of his neck as he let the horse's reins rest lightly over his hand. Dressed in a plain wool tunic in the human style, he looked the most normal out of the brothers. Hugh's own tunic sparkled in the light. Tania had made it for him. He'd asked for clothes that did not tinkle and, though he got ones that did not sparkle as brightly as the other faeries, the dark brown material still glimmered. "We know you have done more than either of us to free her."

"Food," William said, more to himself. He wiggled around on his unseen horse, thrusting a hand out of his sleeve with a piece of dried beef. "Anyone else?"

"Aye." Thomas held out his hand. William leaned over, giving him the piece he'd bitten off of, only to reach inside his robes and grab another. Thomas sniffed the meat before shrugging and putting it in his mouth. Hugh shook his head in denial when William offered him one, not bothering to answer otherwise as he continued with the conversation.

"But it is my duty as the oldest." Pain rolled through Hugh. Thomas had been watching Bellemare. He was doing what he needed to. William searched for a cure, as that was what he needed to do. But, in the end, Hugh knew the responsibility to be his. He was the Earl of Bellemare. He was the head of the family. Banishment from the Mortal Realm and time would never change that. When he saw Juliana's statue, he was reminded of how he failed her.

"You cannot control everything brother." Thomas nudged his horse forward, taking point as they neared a rocky path only wide enough for them to go single file along the steep ledge. They'd ridden for hours from the edge of Feia where Queen Tania had materialized the Silver Palace so they could start their journey as close to the Black Palace as possible. The rolling fields around the faery palace turned into small hills. The small hills grew into larger foothills. And, as the day now turned into evening, the foothills finally rose in the distance to show a range of glorious mountains. They skirted around the edge, following it to where they would find King Merrick.

"I do not try to—" Hugh began.

"And definitely not the will of others," Thomas interrupted him. "Juliana chose her fate, Hugh. No matter how you flog yourself for what has happened, it will never be your fault, nor was it ever your decision to make."

"Juliana may be sweet, but she is strong of will and set in her purpose once she decides it is her purpose," William called from behind. Hugh glanced over his shoulder, frowning slightly.

"Aye," Thomas agreed. "Do you remember when we were younger and she wanted to be a boy so that she might leave Bellemare to train with us?"

"She had no desire to be a knight." Hugh remembered the tiny wisp of a girl standing up to the gruff old earl, their father. She'd refused to eat for a day, promising to never take another bite. Their father, easily swayed by his pretty daughter's manipulations, had relented before the girl felt the first real pangs of hunger. He'd taken her with them to ride to the lord's castle where the boys would train. But, after discovering she'd have to sleep out of doors with a group of obnoxious boys and that the lord's kitchen was overrun with rats, she'd changed her mind.

"Aye, but she wanted to go with us on an adventure. Juliana always resented being a lady because it kept her home." Thomas kept to the side as the path widened. Hugh once more rode up next to him only to have William join them. "All she ever wanted was an adventure and here when her chance came, she seized it."

"All I ever wanted was to keep my family safe," Hugh said. "To live honorably and die a good man."

"And so you shall." Thomas nodded.

"A good faery anyway," William smirked.

"With wings." Thomas leaned back on his seat, staring behind Hugh to where he'd hidden his wings from them with faery magic.

"I knew I would never hear the end of it!" Hugh lightly kicked his horse, sending it forward along the open path. The faery magic went with him, taking the barrier that kept them from the rain. Thomas and William gasped in protest as the chilled water hit their flesh, soaking into their clothing.

"Hugh!" William yelled.

"Come on, Will." Thomas raced after the king. "Never will I say I was outridden by a faery!"

Merrick wasn't sure what he was doing, he only knew he needed to do it. Every bit of his heart and soul called out to the fates, begging them to save Juliana and his son no matter the cost. He'd give his own life for theirs, as unworthy of a trade as it was, if only fate would take it.

The mountain paths took him higher, but Kalen's horse was used to climbing the steep inclines and did not pause as he carried his rider up. Below, in the distance, he saw the rain, but the storm had yet to reach where he was. Instead, fog covered the land, rolling gently over the flowers and grasses, but not so thick as to hinder the way.

He felt the trolls in the nearby caves, living alone in complete isolation and happy that way. They crawled all through the mountain systems, beneath the surface through natural tunnels formed in the earth. On the mountain surface, other creatures roamed. He glanced to the side, sensing creatures in the distance behind a large boulder, near a high rock face that would protect their fire from the evening wind. Merrick avoided them, not needing the council of mountain gnomes or rock faeries, no matter how unblessed they were.

Merrick came to the mountains for one reason, to speak with the troll elder, Fowler. She was the meanest, ugliest creature of the whole race, but she also owed her allegiance to the unblessed crown. And, she had the great talent of locating anything in the Immortal Realm with the magic crystals that grew in her cave.

If anyone could find Ean, Fowler would.

Suddenly, he thought of his brother. Part of his mind constantly concentrated on sensing the Blessed King and Merrick felt the connection pull down the side of a cliff. Merrick reined the stallion hard, causing it to kick out its front legs as it reared up.

Turning, he galloped back down the way he came. Ean was on Valdis land. Perhaps the fates had heard him and had taken pity. Ean being on his land could only be a good sign and Merrick dared to grasp the thin thread of hope that washed over him. Nothing would bring the king of all that was blessed onto his land, not even the war.

"Thank you, fate," he whispered, leaning back so that the horse could make his way swiftly down the mountain. He pushed his magic out toward his brother, concentrating on the thin thread that joined them, willing Ean to hear and come to him. "Anything you want brother will be yours, only help me save them."

They will be saved. They will be saved. They must be saved.

CR80RO

"What was that?" Ean jerked around in his seat as the horse's hindquarters jarred violently to the left. The rain had let up to a drizzle, giving dreary relief to the foul weather. Nerves knotted his stomach and though every fiber of his being urged him to lie to himself, he knew the truth. He was losing Wolfe and this time death was taking him for real.

"I will check." Adal swung from his unicorn, absently patting the beast along its side as he walked back to the cot. Ean glanced around the dark trees. The hour grew late and he'd hoped to have been at the Black Palace before now. He turned, about to speak, only to jolt as Adal swore. "By all that is blessed!"

"What?" Ean jumped from his horse, landing in the sticky mud. His feet squished, clopping and sucking against the slippery land as he trudged to where Adal stood next to Brodor, his fist filled with long hairs. "What is it?"

"They do not look well. Brodor's beard has fallen out." Adal opened his fist and knelt down, working to pull at the straps. "They struggle. Methinks they cannot breathe."

Ean barely glanced in the fallen warrior's direction as he went to Wolfe, automatically reaching for his chest to start releasing the stiff, wet straps. Wolfe's features were corpselike, pale and sunken. Black circles marred the flesh around his closed lids.

"Wolfe," Ean whispered, feeling the heartbeat beneath his hands weaken more. Already it had been faint. This was it. He'd lost. "He's dying."

"Brodor, too." Adal sounded panicked. "I do not know what else we can do."

Ean pulled at the straps, his fingers slipping on the knots as he tried to untie them. Finally, he gave up and reached for the knife in his boot. Franticly, he began slicing open the ties, cutting his way down to loosen the hold on Wolfe.

"He darkens," Adal said. "His flesh. I do not understand how..."

"Darkens?" Ean looked at his brother. Wolfe was still pale.

169

"Fur." Adal's features hardened. "He sprouts dark fur."

From the corner of his eye, Ean saw the man stand. Realizing he'd been so worried about Wolfe he hadn't looked directly at Brodor when he came back, he pushed to his feet to see the fallen soldier. Brodor's face was no longer pale as fine little hairs grew all over.

"What is happening to them?" Adal asked.

"He is turning," Ean said, shaking. As he watched, the fur grew. Brodor's mouth and nose elongated slightly and his lips parted to show dangerously long, sharp teeth. "He turns into one of them."

"This makes no sense. The lycan's bite, it does not do this." Adal shook his head, automatically reaching for his sword. Drawing it, he held it up toward Brodor. Without warning, the warrior's body jerked, moving freely without the straps to bind him down. His dark eyes opened wide, their depths flecked with hints of the glowing blue of the werewolf clans. "We cannot kill him. How can we? He is one of us. A cure—"

"There is no cure," Ean whispered, instinctively knowing it to be true. "King Lucien planned this. The wizard betrayed us. The lycans knew we were coming and yet they waited until after you freed Wolfe from the prison instead of stopping us before. And after they bit these two, they ran off. They did not stay and fight us. They did not give chase."

"Mayhap we merely bested them." Adal's tone was weak and unconvinced.

Ean didn't want to look, but he forced himself to see Wolfe's face. His brother's pale features were slowly sprouting fur as Brodor's had done. A low gurgling roar sounded in the back of Brodor's throat, the beginning rumble of a predator's growl. His body jerked and his bones cracked as if breaking apart. The unicorns pawed the ground skittishly, but the well-trained animals did not run. Ean's breath rasped as he shook his head in denial. "Nay. This is what Lucien wanted. He wanted me to fail Wolfe and I have."

"This is not your doing," Adal asserted.

"I took him from the prison." Ean watched Wolfe's face change, each second like a stab to the heart. The prince's jaw worked, as if biting the air as the fangs grew.

"What choice did you have? To leave him? You said it yourself. He is your brother. How could you not try?"

"Wolfe, I'm sorry." Ean made a move to touch his brother, but Wolfe's eyes opened. His blue gaze glowed eerily, slivering until the unnatural color completely overtook his eyes. "Wolfe?"

Wolfe's eyes moved back and forth rapidly until finally focusing on the Blessed King. His blue eyes shifted with gold flecks, narrowing in what Ean could only hope was recognition.

"Wolfe, fight this. Do not give in. Fight." Ean dropped his blade hand, knowing he'd never attack his brother. How could he? "Wolfe, please."

Brodor roared, jerking violently from the cot. Adal lifted his sword. "Do not make me, Brodor."

Brodor's hands lifted, the nail beds extended with claws as sharp as daggers. He breathed heavily, salivating as he looked at Adal.

"Wolfe," Ean whispered, vaguely aware of thundering hooves as he offered his hand to the shifted prince on the cot. Claws cut through the remaining material that bound the prince down, as he struggled to be free.

"Nay!" came a shout, the voice familiar and unexpected. Brodor instantly fell forward onto all fours. Pawed hands thumped the ground as he pushed forward, running down the path the way they'd come, back toward Hades.

"Defend yourself, Ean," Merrick demanded. A blur of movement darted along the forest path toward them. The unicorns neighed in protest, darting to the side to let the Unblessed King pass. Wolfe turned, snarling as Merrick rode past, sword drawn. "Put silver to the heart!"

Instead of stabbing Wolfe, Ean lurched forward to stop Merrick. "Nay, it's Wolfe!"

"Aye, a wolf. Lucien's lycan." Merrick nearly thrust his blade into Ean, but was able to draw his arm off course at the last instant. "Move so that I may dispatch it back to the hell from which it spawned!"

A distant howl echoed over the forest. Brodor called for Wolfe and the prince leapt into the distance, hurrying away on all fours. Merrick made a move to give chase, instinctively ready to face the fight. Ean grabbed his arm. "Nay, Merrick, it is our brother, Wolfe. The lycanthropes infected him."

Merrick stopped, breathing heavily as he turned back to Ean in disbelief. He looked worn, tired. The usual smirk in his expression was gone, replaced by ultimate despair. Ean felt the anguish hit him, knowing it wasn't nearly as strong as what his brother could feel of the misery. "Wolfe is a...wolf?"

"I found a way into the prison. I—" Ean began. They did not touch, merely stared.

"And you did not send for me?" Merrick growled. The Unblessed King stalked forward and Ean stumbled weakly back, out of his brother's reach.

"We are at war!" Ean defended, helpless over Wolfe and more than ready to fight with Merrick because of it. His whole body ached and he just wanted to be home, back in his Golden Palace surrounded by beauty and life. He wanted to forget his brothers, his failure and knew that nothing would ever take the memory of it from him. "Why would I send for you?"

"Because I know…" Merrick stopped, running his hands through his hair in frustration. "I know darkness. I know Lucien's games. He will not stop until he has taken everything from me."

"Your battle with Lucien is your own." Ean stared Merrick down. Neither of them moved toward the other. "I cannot help you."

"My king." Adal still gripped his sword firmly in hand. "We should go."

Ean nodded once. "Aye. There is nothing more for us here in Valdis."

Chapter Eleven

"You cannot," Merrick whispered, keeping his brother from leaving. The shock of finding Wolfe only to discover him even more lost would have to wait. The fates had led him to Ean.

"And you plan to stop me? Are you mad? You cannot be both blessed and unblessed! That is not how it works," Ean fumed. The Blessed King was worn, but was still as youthful and handsome as Merrick remembered him being. "You took your crown. You should have waited for us to help you, but you ran toward your fate and now you must live it."

"I was blessed." Merrick tried to think of how best to explain, how best to ask. He didn't expect the words to be so thick in his mouth.

"I know, brother, but no more. It is as you told me, death and fate can undo much." Ean had hardened some since he took the throne. It was right and fitting that he should do so. A king, even a blessed one, could not be weak. "You took the reign—"

"Juliana," Merrick interrupted. "I was blessed with Juliana and my son. The unblessed can know a blessing." He pointed toward where Wolfe ran off. "Just as the blessed can know an unblessing."

Ean glanced down the path and Merrick felt him hardening more at the reminder of Wolfe. "You dare to mention them to me? You dare to blame their imprisonment on me? For I see well your accusations, Merrick. If not for you they would never have left Tegwen to stop you from fighting the old Unblessed King."

"You dare to blame me?" Merrick asked. "It is your fault they came after me. You told them where I was going. You fought with them—"

"So it was better that I go along and die as well? Or find myself in the prison, the blessed throne, our legacy abandoned?"

"I have no time for this, Ean," Merrick growled. "You must come with me. My son—"

"A boy?" Ean said, as if finally hearing the fact. "You have a son?"

Merrick shook his head in denial.

"The baby is not yours." Ean nodded. "It would make sense that it is not yours."

"It is mine. I felt his power," Merrick said.

"Felt?" Ean arched a brow.

"The baby is not born. It sleeps in his mother's stomach."

"Dead?" Adal asked softly, reminding both kings that he was there.

"Trapped." Merrick turned his black gaze back to Ean. "I need your help."

Ean hid the shock he had to feel. Slowly, he moved to the empty cot, slicing the ties that held it to the back of his horse. He tossed it to the side of the path. His actions prompted Adal to do the same, though the warrior did not take his gaze from King Merrick.

"She was once your blessed ward." Merrick knew neither man trusted him. And for all his eagerness to force them along in a hurry, he kept his calm.

"And it is your doing that she is no longer such. Her family is blessed and under my protection." Ean went to his unicorn, gripping the mane. "I asked you to free her from whatever game it was you played. I begged you to let her go. Whatever this favor you ask is, the problem is of your own doing and I will not help you."

"You must," Merrick demanded, losing his temper.

"Why should I help you? We are at war!" Ean swung up onto the unicorn's back. He gripped the horn.

"A war you wanted," Merrick argued. "I did not ask for this, any of it. But it has been my burden."

"Me? The war started because of you." Ean glared at him, thinking of all the men he had lost. "You instigated everything and now you think to blame me. You stole Lady Juliana, my blessed ward, and took her into your home."

"I made her my queen!" Merrick's words came out in a screaming rush as they fought. "Need you a nobler gesture than that? Or was it your jealousy that caused you to light the bonfire of war? It was your ego that caused you to shoot the first gold arrow!"

"I shot?" Ean gasped in affront.

"Aye, and now because you did not get my Juliana for yourself, you will not help me to save her? To save my son? She was your blessed ward! Does that mean nothing?" Merrick trembled and knew Ean saw the desperation in him. Even now Merrick tasted Juliana's lips, smelled her fragrance, felt her body on his. His blood stirred to claim her, but he could not. He might never hold her again. "All she wanted was to stop the war you started and now she will die of the spell that holds her trapped. Lucien will kill your nephew as a sacrifice. If you will not help me because I..." Merrick hesitated, touching his heart as he gasped at the pain it felt. "If you will not help me because I love her, then do it to keep Lucien from appeasing the evil magic with the blood of my son and my wife."

"Love?" Ean's tense body drew back. He closed his eyes.

"You once told me I was not dead to you, Ean," Merrick pleaded. "I beg you now, as a brother, please help me save her. If not for me, then for your kingdom. She is my light. Without her, I turn to darkness. Do not let Lucien win."

Merrick knew his brother searched him and he let him in, letting him discover anything he would know.

"I will agree to anything," Merrick said. "Just come with me now to the Black Palace. Already it might be too late."

"You will end the war you started?"

"I did not—"

"And I did not," Ean broke in. "I saw your arrow."

"And I saw your arrow."

"Why would I want a war?" Ean asked. "I have much to gain from peace."

"Lucien," Merrick whispered, nodding in sudden understanding. "He instigated this war. I felt the battles coming, but I did not call for it."

"Then we fight for nothing. All those dead, for nothing."

Merrick reached forward, gripping his brother's arm. "We are still blood, Ean. I feel the goodness in you, the forgiveness. Please, feel whatever of those emotions I have left in me. Come with me to my palace. Help me to save what happiness I am allowed to have in my reign. Only death will free me from the title, but Juliana saves me from myself."

"You do not know what you ask of me," Ean whispered.

"Ean, please. This is my son." Merrick didn't need to tell his brother what that meant. As Unblessed King, he should not be able to father a child. In the history of the unblessed throne, the Unblessed King did not have an heir. The kingdom passed from one king to the other with death. Whoever killed the old king became the new. It was the same for the damned. Only the Blessed King had children to whom he passed his rule.

Mating was hard enough for the elfin race, but for Merrick? With the power he held? It should have been impossible. But then Juliana came.

"Ean." Merrick lowered his voice, stepping closer so that Adal could not overhear. Almost desperate, he willed his estranged brother to understand. "We lost our family. Wolfe and Ladon were thought dead and now they are gone. We are enemies, will always be on some level, made so by an eternity of battle between blessed and unblessed. There can never be a true peace between our kingdoms."

The unblessed, by nature, sought to undo that which was blessed. The blessed sought to mend what was unblessed. The blessed creature gave birth to nature and light. The unblessed took nature and shadowed light. The blessed gave hope. The unblessed created fear. Only death would relinquish Merrick of his throne and without misfortune and suffering, he would cease to be. Without the unblessed, the blessed would cease as well. They were two very different sides to the same world. Ean knew this, just as Merrick did.

"No matter how fortunate I started my life..." Merrick tried to continue.

He was a necessary evil, but in the end he was still evil, held prisoner on the edge of darkness. He was feared, hated, blamed. The wicked thoughts that people carried, their sickening deeds, this was his burden to bear. His very power fed off fear and misfortune. Ean's power fed off happiness and pleasure. Out of the three great kingdoms, Merrick had it the worst. Ean would always know love. Lucien was not affected by hate or death. The Damned King drew pleasure from both.

"Ean, I remember what it was like to know…"

Merrick would know hate but crave love. His reign was made all that worse because he had known what it was like to feel the power that came from happiness, the energy that came from sexual pleasures, from being desired not feared. The Unblessed Kings before him had known mischief and fear and continued to know it after their coronation. But Merrick had known happiness and contentment. He had been loved by his people, his family. To have had it and lost it made his suffering all that much worse, for he would never be content again. That is why he would never know happiness. That is why he would never have a son. His suffering made him a powerful king. But, with his sweet Juliana, he had a taste of that former life. He wanted it back. He needed it. She was his heart.

"Out of all my years, only she has brought me ease," Merrick said weakly, unable to put it into any better words. "When I saw her talking to the children in the mortal world… There was a chance that I would be allowed a bit of happiness in this dismal world and I took it."

"When you first took Lady Juliana from Bellemare, I'd hoped she was special, that she was sent to free you from your dark prison, and now I see that she is." Ean looked at the hand on his arm, putting his own over it. "Promise me that we will end this war neither of us wants and I will help you free your Juliana."

Merrick nodded. "Thank you, brother." Going to his horse, he leapt on its back, ready to ride.

Ean motioned to Commander Adal. The elfin leader eyed Merrick warily. "We go to the Black Palace to help King Merrick."

"I must advise against such a course," Adal said.

"We talk peace," Ean said.

Adal glanced at the Unblessed King, clearly not trusting him.

"You are much better on the field than that fool Gregor ever could hope to be," Merrick said to the commander. Adal merely bowed his head, his eyes boring forward. It was the truth, but that was not why Merrick admitted it. He was trying to put the elf commander at ease. The distrust the man felt was palpable, even to one without magic. He also sensed that Ean trusted him and he didn't want the commander convincing his brother to turn around. "Ah, come, Adal. We did not know each other well in childhood, but we would have had chance to speak."

"Forgive me, king, but childhood was a long time ago." Adal wrapped his hand around the unicorn's horn, ready to ride.

"Charm is not a trait of your kind, is it, brother?" Ean teased, albeit uncomfortably.

"Well, I am unblessed," Merrick admitted. The gap between them wasn't healed, not even close. Years and kingdoms stood between them. It was highly possible such things always would be there, keeping them on opposite sides of the ravine. As if in mutual understanding, they kept silent for the ride. Mending the damage between them could not be forced. Merrick pushed them toward his castle, riding hard as he hoped it wasn't too late.

CB80RO

"Anja, please, come away with me." Juliana held her hand out to the child. She pleaded the girl with her eyes, begging her to take it. She kept her words soft, so they did not echo off the empty great hall. "This place is not what you think."

"Do you not want me, Mother?" Anja pouted. Her arms were out to her sides, keeping her balanced as she walked around the fire blazing in the middle of the stone chamber. Her body disappeared, blocked by the fire as she crossed around the other side. Only her small footsteps were heard until she reappeared, crossing around the front. Unlike the stone flame walls that formed the palace, this center bonfire burned bright and hot. Orange light cast out over the ashen stone like torches in a deep cave, flickering and contrasting the hidden nooks, giving a fearsome cast to each haphazardly carved niche.

The fire was held in place by a giant circular pit in the ground. A perfect circle ringed it, making a wall upon which Anja could play. With the top ledge extending out past the bottom support, Juliana couldn't make out the figures carved into the fire pit's base, only detect hints of their bumpy texture.

Anja stopped with Juliana, but did not move or speak. Batting her eyelashes at the Unblessed Queen, she slowly put her hand into the flames, letting it rest in the fire. "Do not be frightened, Mother. The flames do not burn. They are merely a portal back home. All we have to do is jump."

Juliana shook her head. Her stomach ached, as if the child within her screamed silently for her to hear. Everything inside of her, whether it was immortal magic or mortal instinct, told her to leave the palace. But how could she leave the child behind? "Nay, Anja, come—"

"Nay? You do not want me?" The child's lips quivered.

"Nay, I do," Juliana said, "but it's not safe here. We must go."

"That is what I told you. The dark spirits come for you." Anja again skipped around the center pit of fire. "I can feel them getting closer. We must get out of here."

Juliana glanced over her shoulder the way they'd come. The large, dark hall loomed over them, echoing with the low crackle of the flames. Thick columns gave the impression of long, burnt candles, the melted wax dripping up to the high, uneven ceilings instead of down.

"Jump, Mother, jump," Anja chanted in a sing-song voice.

"Anja, please, come away," Juliana whispered. She felt cold creeping over her spine, tingling and tickling her back as chills worked their way up to her neck. Invisible, icy fingers touched her, like a spirit passing in the stirring breeze. They crept along her arm, glanced her elbow and then let go. "Anja, please..."

C8ह0ह0

"Juliana is here." Lucien grinned, his eyes filled with fire.

Only Ari stood in his hall near the fire pit, her violet eyes darkened with kohl. Three leather, studded belts wrapped low on her hips with a thin thatch of material hiding her sex from view beneath a long, transparent skirt. High boots covered her legs, stopping mid-thigh. For a bodice, two leather cups molded to her breasts held in place with straps—one thick that wound around her neck, two thin which pulled the cups together in front and back. Where the glorious expanse of skin did show, markings were drawn.

"Why are you so sad?" Lucien asked, studying her face.

"Stop trying to discover emotions that are no longer there," Ari said. "Mia is dead."

Lucien felt a stab of disappointment at the words, but did not lay voice to them. "Then what troubles you?"

"Anja," Ari stated flatly. "She may be of pure evil, but I doubt her competence."

"The child has been around and has seen too many evil plots that have come to fruition." Lucien closed his eyes, reaching out his hand to again see if he could sense the Unblessed Queen.

"Then what is taking so long? We've waited for nearly half of an hour. They should be through the portal already."

"Patience, my sweet mistress," Lucien whispered, again detecting the queen. "She steps closer to the flame."

In his excitement, Lucien willed an altar to grow. Chains dangled at each corner and a knife appeared on top.

"Is that for me?" Ari purred.

"Later, if you so wish it." Lucien gave a dark laugh. The magic he would receive from today's deed would be enough to beget an heir to his throne from Ari. One child's death so that his son may live. Ari might not trust Anja yet, Lucien didn't even fully trust the soothsayer, but there was one thing the child knew and that was evil.

༄༅

"Anja, come away at once!" Juliana ordered when pleading with the child did not work. She moved closer to the center fire, ready to jerk the girl down by her arm. "As your mother, I command you to follow me. This place is not safe."

Anja skipped out of the queen's reach. Juliana sighed in heavy frustration, stepping around to follow the girl. Suddenly, she stopped as she saw the far side, the side that had been

Michelle M. Pillow

hidden from her before. A low table, with stone chains carved from the corners, had been placed near the flames. Above it was a knife and, around the gray stone base, tiny carved images of demons sucking the souls from mortals.

Ah, mortals. You can never see things how they are. The words Lord Kalen had once told her now whispered across her mind. She had thought herself wise to the ways of the Immortal Realm, but it seemed in many ways she was still the foolish mortal.

You mortals look with your eyes and hear with your ears, but you are blind and deaf, Merrick's voice added.

"I've seen these before," Juliana said to herself. She turned to the fire pit. Anja was on the other side. Hurrying forward, she got a closer look at the fire pit's base. It had the same carvings. "It all makes sense—the flame walls, the dead land." Juliana stood, her voice lifting as she said, "Anja, we have to go now. This place isn't safe. We're in the Damned King's Fire Palace."

Juliana had never been to the Fire Palace, but she'd seen a stone divining basin the Demon King had once given her husband. It had the same gruesome markings on its base.

"Jump into the fire, Mother!" Anja screamed behind her.

Juliana gasped, surprised that the child could move so fast. She spun around, seeing the angry set of Anja's eyes.

See things for how they are, not as I would have them, she told herself.

"You are a demon." Juliana looked at the child and shook her head, not wanting to believe it but knowing she must. She suspected a part of her knew the truth all along. Merrick and Kalen had said the baby was a boy. They would know.

"Do you not want me, Mother?" the child demanded, stepping closer. Black filled her gaze, sucking all color to leave soulless depths. She came forward, her body jerking strangely

184

with each movement. Her skin reddened with indignation and the soft, blonde ringlets of her hair aged with brittle gray. "Jump in the fire, Mother!"

"Stay back." Juliana eased along the side of the center pit, keeping her eyes on the demonic child. She cupped her stomach. Just a few more steps and she'd be able to make a run for the door. "You are not my baby."

Anja screeched, leaping with supernatural grace through the air. She slammed into Juliana's shoulder, shoving her back. With a cry, the queen hit the stone ledge. Heat from the fire blazed up, trailing toward her. A flame band wrapped about her neck, pulling her back. It seared with its heat but did not break flesh. Juliana screamed as Anja clawed at her face and chest. Another ring of fire wrapped her wrist, as the pit dragged her toward its depths.

Juliana punched Anja in the head, sending the girl flying to the side. Her thin body thudded against the ground. Evil laughter filled the hall as the child pushed up from the floor.

"I like to play with you, Mother," Anja said in her sickening sweet voice.

Juliana blocked her words as she used all her strength to break out of the fire's hold. With a loud grunt, she threw her weight forward, falling to the floor. Her stomach cramped, contracting violently.

Not now, please not now. Stay within awhile longer.

Water ran down the inside of her leg, like someone with a pitcher of warm ale poured it down. Cradling her arm around her stomach, she stumbled across the hall, trying to make it to freedom. A trail of water followed her as she moved, only to let up as the cramping became worse.

"It's started!" Anja called out.

Juliana glanced behind her to see the evil child stalking her. She tried to hurry, once again turning to watch where she was going. A stone figure had appeared to block her path. Juliana screamed, scrambling to get past. It might have been years since she'd seen him, but she'd recognize the Demon King anywhere. Even in stone, his dark, cynical gaze pierced her with dread.

"Too late for you," Anja taunted. "He's here and waiting for you."

Lucien's statue creaked. The stone floor was no longer smooth as each rock shifted out of place to make for uneven travel. Juliana's feet became tangled in her gown as the skirt snagged on a sharp edge of the stone floor. She fell over, weakly crawling away from Lucien's statue.

The statue creaked again. Unlike the others, Lucien moved, slowly coming for her like a man slugging through a knee-high mud pit. His feet dragged along the stone, scraping noisily with each step.

Anja skipped around him, clapping her hands happily. "He comes. He comes. He comes to take your baby!"

Juliana cried, hot tears streaming down her face. This was all her fault. She should have been stronger. She should have stayed with Merrick in the Black Palace where she could be safe.

"Merrick," she sobbed. "Find me, please. I'm sorry. I am so sorry."

"Cry, Mother, cry, we love your tears!" Anja sang.

"Hold your tongue!" Juliana screamed hysterically through her tears. Her stomach cramped, seizing violently. Her wet skirt stuck to the back of her legs. "I am not your mother!"

Another stone figure appeared, this time of a scantily clad woman. She stood still, as if watching King Lucien. Her arms hung down at her sides.

Suddenly, Juliana's back hit stone. She looked around. The main hall had shrunk around her, blocking her in. There was no way out, the door was gone. Only a narrow strip of space separated her from the Damned King. Orange firelight glowed behind him, silhouetting his figure and showing her that the only way out was past him. Lucien leaned over, his arms open, his hands turned toward her. She crouched in a corner, pressed against the unforgiving wall. In the background, a still red Anja stood by the stone woman, watching as Lucien loomed forward.

He had her trapped, but she had to try. Juliana darted forward the best she could in her miserable state of labor. There wasn't enough room to go beside him, so she tried to slip under his legs before the slow stone could catch her.

Anja giggled, hopping up and down as she clapped her hands. "Run, Mother, run, but you will never escape!"

Juliana almost made it through. Her belly bumped Lucien's ankle as she pulled her weight with her arms, reaching forward to crawl out. A stone hand clamped on her thigh and she moaned, kicking to be free. It did no good. Lucien had her and he wasn't letting go. His hands grabbed her leg. Slowly, he turned, forcing her uncomfortably around in the tight space.

Juliana clawed at the wall, trying to find hold. Every time she thought she had it, Lucien's stone grip would pull her away toward the center fire. Her fingers became raw, bleeding until they were useless against the stones.

"Into the fire, Mother, into the flames. Tonight we take your baby and dine on your pain," Anja sang.

Juliana reached for the stone woman's leg. The female statue stepped back, out of her reach, not moving otherwise.

"Into the fire, into the flames!" Anja chanted louder, repeating herself as she hopped up onto the fire's ledge. "Into the fire, into the flames!"

Lucien stopped moving, bending over to get a better hold on her. He let go of her now-bruised thigh only to grab for her wrist. Juliana tried to slap at him, but her body ached. Labor pains racked her and her journey over the jagged floor had left her scraped and bleeding. Her raw skin stung with a constant throbbing.

"No hope, dear Mother, no hope at all. No one can save you," Anja said into her ear.

Juliana growled in outrage, swinging her hand into the child's grayed hair. By sheer will, she pulled the girl forward, throwing her toward the fire pit. Anja screamed, her limbs flailing in the air. And then suddenly, she was gone, her little body disappearing as it entered the pit.

"You go into the flames," Juliana said to the creaking stillness.

Lucien's arm swept under her neck and the other beneath her legs. He lifted her into his unbreakable embrace, stepping up onto the ledge around the fire. Juliana gripped his neck, holding tight in hopes that he couldn't get her off him to throw her in. But, instead of prying her off, the statue jumped with her into the fire. All around her was agony and pain, searing her flesh, boiling her blood, drying the moisture from her skirt. And, as she had no choice but to let the pain take her, she whispered, "Merrick, forgive..."

Chapter Twelve

"I swear I saw him cross our path," William insisted, pointing into the forest in the direction that led away from the palace. "King Merrick is in these woods. We must find him before he gets too far. Going to his palace will do no good if he is not there."

"He will go there eventually," Thomas said.

"But who will let us in?" William asked. "The goblins? I wager he has orders that no one enters unless he's there. The way will be blocked."

"Then we will camp outside his door until we find a way inside." Thomas was close to Juliana, even time could not sever their bond. Knowing that she was in trouble clearly ate at him.

Hugh studied Thomas carefully. The closer they got to the Black Palace, the more anxious he had become. It wasn't the first change the faery king noted in Thomas since his brother had come unexpectedly. Aside from the exhaustion, the differences were subtle, hard to see at first, but they became apparent to one who'd known him all his life.

A hardness had settled into Thomas' face and a burden to his once carefree smile. His eyes did not shine as they once had and they did not linger on any of the pretty faeries that crossed his path in the Silver Palace hall. And then, like the sun's first light peeking over the horizon to introduce a new day, realization dawned on him. Thomas felt the weight of responsibility. His look was the one Hugh had carried for many years. Only after marrying Tania did his burden ease.

"You say you only saw one rider?" Hugh asked William.

"Aye, but I swear it was him." William appeared worried, a great feat for the brother who hardly showed any such cautious emotion. "The wind stirs strangely."

"Methought Tania said the wizards lord over the weather. We can thank your kind for this," Hugh answered.

"I know wizard magic and this is not it. Other forces control this foul change." William looked up at the sky. "I fear what is happening this day. We must find King Merrick. I cannot keep Juliana's voice out my head."

"You hear her?" Thomas looked ready to jump off his horse.

"Only whispers of a memory." William was unconcerned with the threatening stiffness of Thomas' stance. "My senses are telling me to find King Merrick because Juliana needs him. And if she needs him, we need him."

"Most kings will not ride alone when at war, even so close to their castle. The Unblessed King does not appear the foolish kind. We will ride to the Black Palace and inquire of King Merrick there." Hugh urged his horse on, picking up the pace once more. They were close to the palace, he could feel it. "It makes for a better plan than riding all over Valdis trying to find a man on a horse. At least from there we will have a better chance of tracking him."

തഗ൞ൽ

Merrick glanced over his shoulder. He tried to resist, but he couldn't help but study his brother for his reaction as he stepped into his home. Ean's eyes traveled over the dark walls and floor, lingering briefly on the thick crimson tapestries and banners hanging behind Merrick's throne.

"The Blessed King," Iago taunted in a frightful hiss, laughing as King Ean looked around. *"Eee-an."*

"Eee-an," Borc mimicked, the words sounding from the other side of the hall.

"Blesss-ed Eee-an," added another, raspy and low. A figure moved from the shadows, rolling across the hall floor where King Ean didn't look.

"E-an, E-an, Eee-an!" said a voice raspier than the others, the tone higher. Mocking laughter sounded all around, coming from nearly twenty voices.

"What?" Ean asked, frowning as he turned several times to see who spoke.

Aside from their taunts, Merrick heard the goblins' whispering, but they did not show themselves.

"He invites King Ean into the unblessed hall," Merrick heard Tuki say.

"Nay, he captures him. The war is won and we have taken it," Iago told the others.

Adal put his back to King Ean, placing his hand on his sword in warning. Ean looked at Merrick in question. The cackling laughter grew. Merrick felt their uneasiness feeding his power.

"Do not mind the goblins," Merrick said. "They try to scare anyone who steps into the hall. They will not attack without my command."

"Call them away," Adal said.

Merrick frowned, not liking the order in his tone. Nevertheless, he commanded, "Leave us, goblins!"

The creatures scurried off in vocal disappointment, a few still hissing their jeers at the two blessed elves.

"They will not be back." Merrick again led the way across the hall. Two sets of footsteps followed him and he stopped. "Commander Adal, is there anything I may get you while you wait in the hall?" Merrick motioned his hand to the side and a table appeared, filled with food and drink.

Adal glanced at it, shaking his head. He opened his mouth to protest, when Ean held up his hand. Nodding at the table, the Blessed King told his man to stay behind.

"This is an affair for brothers," Ean said. "King Merrick will swear your protection on his life, won't you?"

Merrick smirked, but nodded all the same.

Not happy with the decision, Adal didn't move toward the table as Merrick led Ean to the door behind his throne.

"Now that we are alone..." Ean walked beside him down the passage toward the gardens. "What is this we are doing?"

"Juliana is trapped in stone. I need your blood to free her."

Ean stopped walking. The palace was quiet, hardly a soul stirred inside the walls. Merrick detected Lord Kalen pacing in the high tower where he normally slept. The man would not come down anytime soon.

"Not all of it," Merrick closed his eyes. Ean always expected the worst. "Only a few drops. You can spare that much for the life of my son and wife, can you not?"

"I am here," Ean answered.

"This way. She's in the garden. Stay close to me. The grass is a glamour. If you step on it, you will fall for a very long time." A dark wall encased the area. Merrick crossed over the black cobblestone path toward the arched entryway in the garden, silently willing Ean to hurry. The pointed lancet windows gave off a soft orange glow from within, helping to light their way.

"Are things always so dark here for you?" Ean asked. Moonlight shone from above, the full silvery moon bright in the night sky. Stars spotted the clear heavens, a perfect background to the twisted castle towers above them. The door leading back to the palace disappeared and Merrick felt a small measure of relief that Ean could not escape the garden. Part of him expected his brother to change his mind at any moment.

Merrick kept walking. "Nay, sometimes there are clouds."

"I do not know how you stand it. I have only been here a short time and the depression is making me sick."

"I feel the same with just a thought of seeing the Golden Palace again." Merrick walked straight, ignoring the paths that veered off in several directions.

"Where...?" Ean asked as Merrick didn't turn.

The plants along the walls were withered and neglected. Thorns, as sharp as blades, edged the vines. As Merrick neared, the crimson flowers bloomed on the vines and the stone wall beneath them parted, letting him pass.

"They bleed?" Ean reached toward one feeling the dewy petals.

"Keep up," Merrick ordered. Behind him, the walls closed. Ean swore under his breath. Belatedly, Merrick said, "Watch the thorns. They are sharp."

They made it to the center garden. Merrick's eyes went directly to his wife as the vines enclosed them. His feet hit hard upon the ground as he hurried to her side. Juliana's mouth was open wide in a scream and her dress, which had changed from the one she'd been wearing, was torn at the bodice and along the bottom hem.

"This is her?" Ean asked, eyeing the statue. "She is beautiful."

"Aye. She is."

"What did you do to her?"

"I dared to love her." Merrick touched her stone face before reaching to his chest, willing the knife he carried by his heart to come through his clothing. He gripped the hilt of the jeweled dagger. "The witch said I need the blood of royal brothers on opposing thrones. Both of us need to give it freely."

"Why this?"

"Juliana thought she was doing the right thing. She hoped to repair—" he paused, sighing. Taking the knife, he cut his hand, slashing through his palm. Blood ran down his hand, but he didn't let on that it hurt. "She thought she could end my suffering by mending our brotherhood and ending the war. She did this to force my hand, only she was betrayed."

"I'm jealous," Ean held out his hand, "that you have found a woman who would go to such lengths."

Merrick couldn't speak. Somewhere, his wife was in pain. He took Ean's hand in his bleeding one and lifted the blade.

"Make it fast—" Ean began, only to be cut off when Merrick didn't hesitate to cut him. The blade sliced easily through his palm. Merrick let go of his brother. Ean lifted his hand to touch Juliana. Pausing inches from her arm, he looked down to the Unblessed Queen's stomach. "You must trust this witch you speak of very much to listen to her."

Merrick's hand lifted only to stop, not touching her. "I don't trust her, but I trust Lord Kalen and he said to do this."

Ean tried to reach forward, but Merrick stopped him.

"Wait, give me a moment to think."

"What's to think about?" Ean asked. "She's your wife."

Merrick stepped back. "I don't trust the witch. She would only tell me enough to do damage. When Kalen read her, he mentioned the baby being overdue. He said if Lucien..."

Merrick went to the statue, kneeling before her. He put his cheek against her stomach. The stone was warm.

"If Lucien takes the baby, it will kill her. Free from the prison or not, evil will win this way. That is what the witch has to gain. If the queen dies, she'll take my pain over it. There will possibly be enough power for her to escape."

"Then what do you want to do?" Ean asked.

Merrick leaned back, holding up the knife. Drawing back his arm, he hit it against the stone stomach. It chipped, but didn't crack. "Find a rock. Help me."

"Are you sure?" Ean asked.

Merrick's hand shook. He was careful not to get his blood on the stone. "I hope so."

Ë਍ಠ૭

"*Ahh,*" Juliana moaned, grabbing her stomach as pain racked every inch of her body. She was sure the fire would burn her alive, and for a moment it felt like it was, but they passed through it unharmed. Her vision swam, everything on the other side of the fire was a blur. All she knew was that the stone hands holding her had turned into cold flesh when they came out of the heat.

"Cut it from her," Anja's voice ran out. "Make her bleed. She's dying anyway."

"Quiet, Anja," a woman's voice ordered.

"Do not cross me, Ari," Anja warned.

"Anja!" King Lucien growled.

"I do not answer to her," the child pouted. "Now cut her, my king, before it's too late."

Lucien laughed, a dark and vicious sound. "She will not die here. This alternate realm is protected by magic. It's the only way I could draw them both out alive. She won't have the baby until I take her out of it, or until we take it."

Anja giggled. Juliana moaned louder, her jaw working as she tried to speak. She felt tapping against her stomach and the fear that they were going to take her son made her voice finally break free. She screamed, thrashing on the hard, flat bed.

"What is happening to her?" the female voice asked, not as joyous as the other two. "Her stomach is bleeding."

"I haven't touched her," Lucien said.

"Do not look at me," Anja protested. "I am over here."

"She is weakening," the Demon King said.

"Nay," the woman said softly. "She is dying. You are losing her."

CR☙☜⬠

"Ah!" Merrick yelled, beating his wife's stone stomach, trying to break through.

Ean stood behind him, not helping to fracture the pregnant belly. He'd merely said, "I will not hit her, Merrick. If you are wrong, the fault of her death and that of the child will not be mine."

Suddenly, a loud break sounded over the garden. The stone cracked, a jagged trail breaking open from between her stone thighs to her chest. Water pinkened with blood ran out over his hands. Merrick pulled at the stone, chipping at the crack with his fingers.

"I see something," he grunted. On his knees before her, he clawed at the stone, his fingers slipping in the wetness. "Ean, help me."

Ean was by his side, pulling at Juliana's stomach. Together they broke a hole through the stone. A baby's bloody foot popped out only to withdraw back in.

"My son," Merrick cried, seeing that the baby was alive. He ripped a piece of the statue away. A loud wail echoed out of the stone. "My son."

Reaching into Juliana, he pulled the baby out. The wet bundle squirmed in his hands as he pulled it to his chest. Already he could see it had his mother's dark brown hair, but when the baby blinked, Merrick saw his own black eyes staring back at him.

"Merrick," Ean whispered. "What about her?"

Merrick looked at the broken statue. Tears threatened to spill over, as he stood. Thrusting the child at Ean, he ordered, "Hold my son."

Ean took the baby, making a weak noise as he held it. Merrick frantically looked around for Juliana's dagger, only to find it on the ground where he'd dropped it. Crawling toward it, he picked it up.

"Please, Juliana," Merrick whispered, drawing the blade hard against his hand. The first wound had started to heal and he wanted to make sure she had enough blood to come back to him. Looking at his brother, he said, "Ean, your hand!"

Ean hesitated, as he stared down at the child.

"Ean!" Merrick pleaded.

Holding the crying baby with one arm, the Blessed King offered his palm to his brother. Merrick cut it open once more and together they touched the statue—Ean on Juliana's arm and Merrick on the top of the crack, right above her heart.

"Please, Juliana, please," Merrick pleaded. "Take me instead, fate, take me. Not my Juliana."

The stone trembled beneath them. Ean's arm tightened as he held the baby tighter. Then, suddenly, the stone beneath their hands crumbled into a pile of dust. She was gone.

"Nay!" Merrick screamed, causing the child to wail louder at the sound. He reached for the dust, trying to pull it to his chest before the breeze swept it away. "Juliana, nay. I have killed my wife. I have killed her."

"Merrick, we need to get your son inside," Ean urged. "We need to clean him up."

Merrick saw his son in his brother's bloody hands. That was the vision he'd had of the future. "Hands and blood."

"Merrick?" Ean asked, slowly stepping back.

"That is what Kalen and I both saw." This time the tears did fall, spilling down his cheeks.

"Merrick, we need to go inside." Ean's tone was calm, though his expression was strained. "Don't you think Juliana would want you to care for your son?"

"Aye." He nodded, knowing Ean spoke the truth. "But what can I, the king of all that is unblessed, do for him? I have killed his mother."

"The woman you described to me, the woman you love, sounds like the type of woman who would want you to take her life for her son's. You did the right thing, brother."

Merrick wasn't sure how, but he managed to stand. Juliana's voice echoed in his brain, a speechless tone he always carried with him. He saw her face clearly, floating in his memories, memories he would forever keep close to his heart.

"My Juliana," he whispered as the vines parted and closed as they walked through. "I am so sorry I could not save you. My perfect Juliana."

Chapter Thirteen

"We heard a child crying." King Hugh rushed forward as Ean and Merrick entered the great hall of the Black Palace. The Unblessed King tried to be strong, but Juliana's three brothers were the last people he ever wanted to see. All three of the Bellemare brothers bowed to them when they saw the Blessed King, though the action was weak and rushed. Hugh searched both men, only to stiffen when he saw the baby in Ean's arms. "Is that?"

"My son," Merrick said weakly. His magic automatically searched for her, but all he felt was his son where her power used to be. The child already was a powerful being and Merrick could only guess that his magic would grow stronger in time.

"A son?" Thomas whispered, going toward the child. "It is over? The curse is lifted?"

"The way was open," William explained.

Merrick didn't move. He'd forgotten to close the entrance when he led Ean and Adal into the hall.

"Where is Juliana?" William asked, searching behind Merrick to look down the hall.

Merrick felt Ean's eyes on him, but what could he say? He felt as if his heart had been ripped from his chest and in its place was the echoing reminder of his loss. His nose burned, but he did not cry. How could he? He had to be strong for the only part of his wife that was left.

"What have you done, Merrick?" Hugh pointed at the Unblessed King's bloodied hands. The wounds had healed shut on the elfin king's palms, but Merrick did not will the crimson reminder of what had happened away. He did not clean himself, did not change his attire.

"King Merrick, please, where is our sister?" Thomas asked.

Merrick opened his mouth to speak, but no sound came out. Deliberately, he shook his head once. The brothers' faces fell. The smell of food drifted over the hall, coming from the banquet table he'd procured for Commander Adal. The commander stood next to it, back from the others, watching what happened.

"Nay," Thomas whispered, stumbling back as if Merrick struck him. He grabbed his heart. "It cannot be. Not Juliana."

Hugh stood still, his body tense, his eyes hard. He said nothing, merely stared at the Unblessed King. Merrick felt his hate of him.

"Her child..." William mumbled incoherently to himself as he went toward Ean. He held out his hands. "Please, may I see the boy?"

The wizard took the child, pulling out his wand. Murmuring low incantations, he blessed the child, cleaned and swathed him in a thick cloth. The baby instantly settled.

"What happened?" Hugh demanded.

"She didn't make it back. We did all we could, but we could only save the child," Ean answered.

Merrick closed his eyes tight. Ean lied. It was Merrick's fault that Juliana did not make it. He was the one who decided to take the baby out of her. But if he hadn't, wouldn't the child have died? Was that the price fate had wanted him to pay as Unblessed King? He had to pick one life over the other and fate would make him live with that.

Why had he brought Juliana to his world? He should have just left her in the mortal realm where she was safe. Magic, curses and Kings of the Unblessed didn't exist in the mortal world. If he had left her there, she'd be safe now.

Pain ripped through him in continual waves. Even now he knew he could never have left her alone. She was his air, his life and now that she was gone so was his heart. He didn't know what to do, so he just stood. Only the thought of his son kept him from ending his own life.

"I want you to let me take Juliana's son with me," Hugh said. "He shouldn't grow up here. Our sister didn't belong here and neither does her son."

"I'll take him to Bellemare," Thomas said. "To the mortal world."

Hugh glanced at his brother and nodded. "Aye, Bellemare. He'll be safe there."

"And when his magic grows?" Merrick asked.

"Then I will take him to Feia, to the faeries. We know magic and he will be loved and well cared for." Hugh looked at the child in William's arms. He motioned to the wizard to bring the baby to him. "It is what his mother would have wanted."

"I—" Merrick began, not knowing exactly what he was going to say. The baby would be safer at Feia, but the idea of losing him was too much.

"Really, Hugh? Is that what I would have wanted?"

"Juliana?" William and Thomas gasped in unison.

"What?" Hugh breathed in surprise.

Merrick was afraid to believe he heard the low, soft lullaby of her voice. He watched her come into the great hall from the direction of the stairwell that led abovestairs to their bedchamber. He tried to feel her power with his own, but it wasn't there. It was as if she were truly gone. If this was a dream, if she wasn't real, he didn't want to wake up.

Juliana looked almost like she had when he'd first laid eyes on her, those long years ago. She'd captured his notice one night as he flew through the mortal realm disguised as a falcon. Just like he did then, he now watched her walk toward him like a play. From that first moment, he loved her, as much as any creature could love. He hadn't wanted to fall for her, but he had.

Her long dark hair spilled in waves over her shoulders, so soft he wanted to bury himself in it for an eternity. Wide blue eyes stared into his soul and he let them. He was nothing without her and he couldn't hide a single thing when he looked at her. She was his goddess and Merrick would let her have free use of him, for good or ill.

Her white gown sparkled like faery cloth, so light it fluttered with each movement. More than a queen, more than an angel, she came to him—a perfect vision of his heart.

"Give me my son," Merrick said, his voice hoarse. Without taking his eyes from her, he went to Hugh. "Give him to me."

Hugh handed the baby over. Merrick hugged the child to his chest, crossing to where his wife was. Cradling the baby in one arm, he lifted a shaking hand toward her. He hesitated before touching her, staring into her eyes, willing her to be real. She looked down at the baby, her smooth cheek so close to his hand.

"Juliana," he whispered, forcing his hand to move. His fingers met with flesh and his heart thumped hard, coming back to life. In that second, he felt her again with his magic, felt her presence, felt her as surely as he felt himself. The power in her had shifted, no longer as strong as it had been in pregnancy, but still there under the surface. "Oh, Juliana."

Merrick let out a weak sob of relief, pulling her forward to his chest. He didn't care if tears streamed his face, if he cried out loud, or if the goblins saw how he loved his queen. Love poured over him, filling his dark soul with the pleasure and light of the perfect moment. The baby was crushed between them but he was careful not to hurt his son.

"Merrick, Merrick," she whispered, over and over, his name like a song he'd never tire of.

"Methought I lost you." Merrick cupped her face. "Methought you were dead. I saw your ashes. Methought I killed you. What happened? Where were you? Oh, I do not care, just never leave my side again. Naught matters but us, right here, right now."

"Merrick, the goblins, they were in the hall. If they hear you—" she began.

"Let them hear," he drew back, leaning his head back as he raised his voice. "Let them all hear! I love you, my perfect wife, my Juliana, my queen, my heart, my life, my everything. I love you."

And then, as the echoes of his declaration died, something amazing happened. Nothing. There was no rush to claim his throne. The goblins did not revolt. His powers did not weaken. Everything was as he'd always hoped it could be.

"I love you," he said again. His bloodstained clothing dirtied hers, staining the pretty white. "I love you."

Juliana grabbed him by his tunic, shaking him hard. "What took you so long to get me? Methought you would never come."

"You trusted the witch from the dungeon. She is evil. She betrayed us both."

"But, she had your blood. Why?" Juliana frowned. She again looked down at their son, smiling as if she couldn't stop herself. "I cannot believe he is safe. When I awoke in our bedchamber without magic, methought he was lost. I feared Lucien had got him." Then touching the baby's cheek, she said, "So you are the precious angel that's been kicking me for so long."

Merrick shifted his arm so Juliana could hold the child. She clutched him to her chest, not stepping away from Merrick. A tear slipped down her rosy cheek, dropping onto the swaddling cloth William had given him.

"Juliana?" Hugh said behind them. "What is happening?"

Merrick moved so Juliana could see her brothers standing behind him. He'd forgotten they were there.

"Hugh." Juliana grinned. "Thomas, William! I'm so glad you are here. I have missed you." She turned, smiling around at everyone in the great hall. "I have missed all of you." Then, eyeing Ean, she said, "Well, not you. I do not know you." Adal caught her attention. "Or you. My apologies, but I promise to miss you later."

"Juliana, are you well?" Thomas asked.

"Now I am." Her happy smile shone on Merrick. "Now I am perfect. He has saved me and our son. Come see your nephew, Thomas. You, too, Will and Hugh. Tell me how beautiful he is."

Her three brothers surrounded Juliana and the baby. Merrick stepped back to Ean. Holding out his hand, palm out, he said, "I cannot thank you enough, brother. You have given me my heart back."

To Merrick's surprise, Ean didn't return the happy look. Sadness edged his eyes, darkening them slightly. He didn't lift his hand.

"Ean?"

"You cannot know all that has happened and do not ask me to tell you," Ean said.

"What do you know? Is—?" Merrick started to speak.

"It is not your son or your wife. It is none of that. In fact, it does not concern you." Ean put his hand up to Merrick's, pressing palm to palm. "I am happy for you, brother, for your blessing. Take care of them for I can never help you again. You have already taken everything from me. I have nothing left to give you."

Merrick frowned at Ean's enigmatic words. "Is this about Wolfe? If there is a cure, we will find it."

"There is not. You know as well as I do. All we can do is hope that he does not follow the path of evil. Those of the lycan kind have done it before." Ean glanced away. Neither one of them mentioned the fact that, in the one case they knew of, the lycan woman had been torn apart by her fellow wolves.

"Is it the peace you worry about? I will not go back on my word. I will call the men off."

"The peace stands. It will take us both some time to convince our sides of it, yours more than mine I imagine, but we will start on the path." When Merrick started to pry into Ean's cryptic meaning, his brother lowered his hand. "Now, introduce me to your wife. I should like to meet my former blessed ward."

CB8OB0

"Methinks we should call him Kynan Alwyn for the old Blessed King," Juliana said.

"Alwyn? For our grandfather?" King Ean asked in surprise.

"He was the one who blessed my family. And Kynan, which means chief. He will be a great man. I feel it." Juliana smiled at King Ean. She should have known him by his looks, but the truth was, she was still overwhelmed by her ordeal in the Fire Palace.

One moment, she was being held down on a table with her stomach ripped open and bleeding, the next she was on her bed—alone, disoriented and no longer with child. But then, she had heard something. A baby cried and she knew her child was alive. Warmth washed over her, sparkling around her like the night stars and she found herself in a beautiful gown, floating toward the bottom of the stairs. Air passed through her, tickling her insides. Seeing Merrick, even though red stained his clothes and hands, her heart sped and she couldn't reach him fast enough. She'd longed for the look of his dark eyes, piercing her, full and solid. Only when Merrick touched her did her body right itself once more. She was where she belonged, at home, with him.

Juliana looked at her husband. He nodded. "A fine name."

"I cannot thank you enough for what you have done," Juliana said to Ean.

"I suppose I should thank you for going to such lengths to end this war," the Blessed King answered.

Though he smiled, Juliana detected a sadness in the king. Though the feeling fed her power as such things had before, her body was calmer.

"We must go," Ean said. "The encampment will be expecting us back."

"Thank you," Merrick said.

Michelle M. Pillow

Ean nodded, motioned to his commander and strode from the hall.

"Juliana?"

She turned to Hugh. He waved her to the side, leading her away from the others so they could speak in private. "What is it, Hugh? You cannot honestly be upset that I am not letting you take my son. I know you do not like Merrick, but—"

"We thought he killed you." Hugh's eyes searched hers, as if he could discover some secret in her. "I worried that you had cast yourself into stone because of me. We know how important family is to you. My hatred of Merrick..."

Juliana touched Hugh's arm when he paused. "Of course, I want my family at peace. You are my brother, Hugh. Nothing will change that, not marriage or time. You did not do this to me. You are not at fault. I cannot explain why exactly that I did this, but methinks it was to have peace in my home. The baby is powerful and there is so much good in him. Methinks his power overwhelmed me until all I could think of was peace. I needed peace in this realm."

"But you are used to war. Juliana, you grew up around it," Hugh said.

"Methinks it was my son who wanted it most," she whispered.

"Kynan? But, how can that be?"

"You should know by now, brother, that nothing in this realm is what it seems." She looked over to her family—Thomas, William, Merrick—all focused on her child. "My son is so powerful, but he can handle it. He will grow to know his magic. Methinks what I felt was some sort of magical pregnancy sickness. I felt so much that my mind could not handle the rush. The more the baby grew, the stronger it was. What I did, I did for Kynan. Or mayhap because of him. I'm not really sure."

208

"You know that I try…" Hugh hesitated, but he didn't need to say more. Juliana understood.

"I know." She touched his arm. "I know you do not like him because you love me. I understand and would not change the fact that you love me, not for anything. Methinks, you will come to respect Merrick in time, perhaps even see him as a brother. But, if anything, as immortals we have time."

CRITICAL

"I have served under you long enough to know when something is very wrong, my king," Adal said as they slowed their mounts. They rode hard and fast from the Black Palace. Ean couldn't help it. He had to get away.

"It is naught," the king said. "The unblessed powers do not sit well with me."

"Nor I," Adal agreed. "Forgive me for prying, but there is something else, isn't there? When you two were gone, I felt a strange shift in my bones. The baby, is he—?"

"It's not the baby," Ean said softly, "at least not in the way you think. The baby is as any other creature, only with strong magic. There is the ability to be both good and evil in him."

"Then what is it?"

Ean looked at his trusted friend, perhaps the most trusted friend he had. Pain rippled over him, hard and heavy as it stuck in his chest. "It took a great blessing for that child to be born and we all know that magic comes with a price."

"And the price of Kynan's birth?" Adal frowned, studying the king intently.

"My future," the Blessed King said. "The price was my future. To bless the unblessable, magic took my future child, my future wife and happiness as trade. When I helped him free his family, fate took mine from me. I felt it being ripped from my destiny, as real and as agonizing as my heart being ripped from my chest. Merrick will now have the family life that should have been mine." Ean lifted his jaw, trying to fight down the pain. "He has taken everything from me. I have nothing left but my rule. But, considering I have the throne that should have been his, perhaps this is just."

"Are you certain?" Adal's unicorn pranced nervously, feeding off the anxiety of its rider. "Mayhap, the unblessed presence drained you. Mayhap..." The commander looked helplessly around, as if the trees could tell him some answer.

"I knew before Merrick even asked that for him to have a son would take my sacrifice. A trusted light wizard foretold it." Ean held up his hand, stopping Adal from speaking more. "I knew what I gave up and I know what I took in assuming the throne. Fate can be a cruel mistress to us all, but this is the destiny she has chosen for me."

CB8O8O

Lucien glared at Anja, his hands still covered with Queen Juliana's blood. Stalking her around his hall, he threw a stone block in her way, causing her to jump and run around them.

"Do not blame me, my king!" The child's voice rang playfully. She might be angry with him, but she was still enjoying his temper.

Ari watched, as she had through the whole ordeal, not sure what to feel. The new darkness in her stung with acute disappointment that such a powerful surge of energy to the Damned throne would be lost. The old light rejoiced. She hid the light from Lucien, doing her best to smother it out. Still, there were times when it tried to peek through, when she couldn't suppress it and she became glad that the Unblessed Queen and her child were safe.

"She did it!" Anja pointed to where Ari stood. Ari stiffened, worried about how much the child suspected. "And you! This is your fault. Your weakness for her is weakening your rule. Send Ari back to the dungeons where she belongs. Let me show her the true depths of what our hell can be."

Fearful that the soothsayer would reveal her deeds, Ari hurried forward, grabbing the child as she tried to run past. Anja yelped in surprise at being caught. Ari held her up, gripping her little dress with both hands.

"I know it was you who sent the knife to Merrick," Anja whispered.

Ari glanced at Lucien to see if he had heard. He was coming for them, but his expression hadn't changed. His annoyance continued to direct itself at the child.

"Take her!" Ari threw the soothsayer down hard. "Put her in the dungeon. Her visions are clearly useless, otherwise she'd have seen this. She would have known."

"My visions are—" Anja cried.

"Are pathetic," Ari yelled at her. Pouting her lower lip, she swung her hips as she moved toward Lucien. "Put your little pathetic doll away, Lucien. I have much bigger games to play with you."

"Aye?" He quirked a brow, his gaze dark with wonder.

Running her hand over his chest as she passed him, she went toward the altar. "Aye. You promised to chain me down, if it was my will." She sat on the stone ledge, still bloody from the failed deeds. Slowly, she rolled down to her back, lifting her hands over her head. "It is my will, Lucien."

The chains snapped up in response to his biting desire, locking over her wrists and pulling her down hard. With a harsh wave of his hand, he slapped Anja with his power, sending her flying across the room. She slammed into a wall with a heavy thud. The soothsayer only laughed. Lucien swiped his hand again and this time her body squashed into the floor, disappearing as he sent her back to the bowels of the palace.

"Leave her there." Ari's eyes narrowed as she commanded and begged Lucien at the same time. She parted her thighs in invitation. "She is of no use to us."

"Us?" The Damned King stood before her bound body, looking down as the clothes melted off her form.

"You and me, Lucien." Ari arched her back, thrusting her breasts up as she pushed toward him. "Us."

꧁꧂

"Are you sure there is nothing we can do for poor Kalen?" Juliana asked, stroking the dark locks of her son's head. The baby slept on their bed, nestled perfectly between them. Though tired, she didn't want to close her eyes only to discover that she was dreaming. "We owe him much."

"Leaving him alone in his tower chamber, away from everyone, is the best we can do for him. He will have to work out of the madness in his own time." Merrick touched Kynan's back, almost petting him as he ran his fingers over the supple flesh. They'd talked for hours, about everything that had happened, saying everything that needed to be said.

"And the old witch? She should be punished for betraying us." Juliana put her hand over Merrick's and squeezed.

"She will be. Ean has agreed to take her once the war is officially ended and he will lock her away in the Golden Palace's prison, surrounded by happiness and light. She will have nothing to feed on and will lose all her powers because of it." Lifting her hand, Merrick gently kissed it. "The old crone will never hurt anyone again."

"You never told me how she got your blood." Juliana pushed up from where she laid, lifting Kynan into her arms. Sitting on the bed, she rocked her son.

"I traded it to her for something more important."

"And what was that?" Juliana could tell he wanted to lie to her.

"Thomas' life. It was the only way to save him."

"That first day of battle," Juliana said in understanding. "He did die, didn't he?"

"Aye. His horse crushed his body. The witch was the only one who could save him. I knew the risk when I made the trade. I knew the power I was giving her."

"Then why did you do it?"

"Because it is what you would have wanted of me, my queen. As I told you that night long ago when you first came here, I do not rearrange my world for just anyone." Pushing up to join her in sitting, he cupped her cheek, leaning in so his lips were brushing against hers. "But for you, I would take the very stars from the sky. I am yours, my love, completely and utterly yours. All you have to do is ask it and I will do your bidding."

Her heart filled with the perfection of the moment. Merrick loved her. She had always known, but to hear the words, to hear them said so sure and clear, made her body heat and her heart overflow. "I love you, too, my king, my reason for living."

Merrick kissed her, crushing his lips to hers. His tongue edged into her mouth, wet and warm. She moaned, needing to feel him. They had spoken of so much since her return, but they had yet to fully touch.

"How do you feel?" he asked. "Women, after babies are born, they are…"

"I am not a mere woman and our child was born in a…" She paused searching for the right word. Before she could think of it, he interrupted.

"So you are saying your body…? We can…?" The wicked grin spreading over his lips said it all. "I have been holding back because methought you ill."

"And here methought you wanted to talk." She gave a pretend frown.

"Well, aye, I do, but, I also want to…" He looked down her body in meaning.

Juliana tossed her head back, laughing. They'd been speaking quietly as Kynan slept and the boy now jarred, fussing as he opened his eyes.

"You said I could ask for anything and you would give it?"

"Aye, my love, just ask it." He gazed at her and she felt his desire threading through the air.

Juliana looked to the side. "How about a bed for him? But make it close. I want him in the room with us, at least for now. I do not want him out of our sight."

Merrick smiled, lifting his hand. A bed grew from the stone with sides forming like bars around the edges. The blunt tips reached high, bending inward around the center. In the middle an oval mattress grew, covered with a soft material.

"A cage?" Juliana asked.

"A safe place," Merrick corrected.

Juliana smiled, standing beside their bed. Merrick moved his hand, motioning toward the bed so she could see how it opened. A door swung forward and she set the baby inside. Kissing her fingers, she placed them to the baby's head before pulling a blanket over Kynan. She shut the door, latching him safely in.

Instantly, Merrick's hands wrapped around her from behind. "Do not worry, the baby cannot hear us."

Juliana's clothes dissolved and she gasped as his hot, naked flesh pressed against her back. His hands brushed over her, one gliding over the soft curls, back and forth, back and forth, pressing deeper into the folds with each pass. The other found a breast, squeezing gently. She opened her mouth wide, gasping as she turned to face him.

Merrick pulled her onto the bed, his body lying next to hers. Wiggling her hips, Juliana tried to anticipate his movements, forcing him more firmly against her. His finger encircled her sex and she weakly cried out, the sound swallowed by his hovering mouth. He breathed into her, harsh and loud.

Wet with her cream, he slid his finger along her opening with precision. Merrick thrust a finger inside.

"Oh," he breathed, biting his lip. Firelight illuminated his handsome face, giving heavy contours to his chiseled features. "Ah, how I have missed holding you."

With a groan, he kissed her mouth, taking it hard as his tongue delved deep only to pull back. The movement mimicked the finger inside her, moving in and out, in and out, faster, deeper. The thickness of his finger grew, as if suddenly there were two stroking her sex intimately. Pressure built and he pulled his mouth back with a soft growl.

"I need to feel myself within you," he said.

"Take me, Merrick, I need you," she answered.

He rubbed the tip of his erection along her wet folds, following the path his finger traveled moments before. Pushing her legs open, he swiftly delved into her, imbedding himself fully. She yelped in surprise as her muscles were stretched around his thick arousal.

"Finally," he whispered.

Juliana giggled. Merrick pulled his hips back, rocking in short, deep thrusts. Juliana let him take control as she was left with the beginning sensations of pleasure. His movements became bolder and she sprung into action. She moaned in protest as she wrapped her legs around the backs of his. Using all of her strength she forced him to thrust into her again, this time even deeper. The eager motion brought with it throbbing gratification. She loosened her legs to instinctively do it again. She could not have stopped if she wanted to.

Driven by the primal need for release, her head turned from side to side on the bed in sweet torment. Merrick grabbed under her knees and forced her legs further apart. His finger moved to her sex, rubbing along the hard bud. Sensation after astonishing sensation washed over Juliana. Her body tensed, building with each of his thrusts. She moaned in encouragement, mindless of anything but the man on top of her. Without warning he tensed between her thighs, pressing one last hard time into her. Juliana's body joined his, quaking with an inner force so great she swore she fell off the edge of the earth.

෫෫ඁ෪

"Sh," Gorman hissed, crawling past the end of the bed where the king and queen slept. "Do not bother them."

"I'm not bothering them. You are the one talking. I am doing my duty. You heard our queen." Halton put his hand over his heart, even as he poked his hand between two rails. "She wants us to stand guard over the baby. He is our duty now."

"Actually, she said, 'I do not want him out of our sight'," Gorman corrected.

"That is what I said. We all—you, me, King Merrick and our sweet Queen Juliana, but mostly me. We are to keep a sharp eye on the baby." Halton turned his head, staring down at the child with one eye. Kynan slept, completely undisturbed.

Gorman squeezed through the side rail of the bed, rolling next to Kynan. "Oh, soft."

"Aye?" Halton followed suit, curling next to the boy's other side. "Oh, aye."

"I can watch him better from here." Gorman yawned.

"Aye," Halton said. "I can."

"I said, I can," Gorman whispered.

"I can," Halton said under his breath.

"Me. They told me."

"Me."

"Me."

Halton yawned, drifting asleep. "Nay, me."

About the Author

Michelle has always had an active imagination. Ever since she can remember, she's had a strange fascination with anything supernatural. She is married (madly in love) and has a wonderful family. To learn more about Michelle M Pillow's Samhain Publishing titles or the Realm Immortal series, please visit her website at www.michellepillow.com. Send an email to Michelle at michelle_pillow@yahoo.com or join her Yahoo! Group to learn of upcoming and current releases! http://groups.yahoo.com/group/michellempillow/join

Look for these titles

Now Available

Realm Immortal: King of the Unblessed
Realm Immortal: Faery Queen
Talons: Seize the Hunter
Talons Print Anthology by Mandy M Roth,
Michelle M Millow, Sydney Somers, Jaycee Clark and
Shannon Stacey

Will this Elven warlord be conquered by lust?

Lords of Ch'i
© 2006 Ciar Cullen

Cast out by an usurper to her clan's throne, warrior Silver SanMartin throws herself at the mercy of her compelling enemy, Jet Atraud. The sexy warlord rules his Elven clan with an iron fist, but Silver finds she lords some power of her own. Jet can't keep his eyes—or his hands—off his lovely captive.

In a battle to gain self-control and maintain his ten-year oath of celibacy, Jet tries to focus on the task at hand— conquering the enemy clans. Despite his strong will and best intentions, Jet cannot ignore his growing love for Silver. But can a sworn enemy be trusted?

Available now in ebook and print from Samhain Publishing.

Discover the Talons Series

5 STEAMY NEW PARANORMAL ROMANCES
TO HOOK YOU IN

Kiss Me Deadly, by Shannon Stacey
King of Prey, by Mandy M. Roth
Firebird, by Jaycee Clark
Caged Desire, by Sydney Somers
Seize the Hunter, by Michelle M. Pillow

AVAILABLE IN EBOOK—COMING SOON IN PRINT!

WWW.SAMHAINPUBLISHING.COM

hot stuff

Discover Samhain!
THE HOTTEST NEW PUBLISHER ON THE PLANET

Romance, fantasy, mystery, thriller, mainstream and more—Samhain has more selection, hotter authors, and everything's available in both ebook and print.

Pick your favorite, sit back, and enjoy the ride!
Hot stuff indeed.

WWW.SAMHAINPUBLISHING.COM

GET IT NOW